The "Good" Reverend

*'Was he a saintly man or
was he a man who practiced false piety'*

Herman Edel

THE "GOOD" REVEREND

iUniverse books may be ordered through booksellers or by contacting:

iUniverse LLC
1663 Liberty Drive
Bloomington, IN 47403
www.iuniverse.com
1-800-Authors (1-800-288-4677)

Because of the dynamic nature of the Internet, any web addresses or links contained in this book may have changed since publication and may no longer be valid. The views expressed in this work are solely those of the author and do not necessarily reflect the views of the publisher, and the publisher hereby disclaims any responsibility for them.

Any people depicted in stock imagery provided by Thinkstock are models, and such images are being used for illustrative purposes only. Certain stock imagery © Thinkstock.

ISBN: 978-1-4917-3815-3 (sc)
ISBN: 978-1-4917-3814-6 (e)

Library of Congress Control Number: 2014910862

Printed in the United States of America.

iUniverse rev. date: 08/05/2014

The Pavlac Legacy, Scrambled Eggs and Mashed Potatoes, Taormina, and The White Gospel Singer are previous works of Mr. Edel.

Chapter One

A huge roar of laughter burst from Anthony Angus Donnell. Fortunately, as he was sitting alone in his garden, no one was near enough to hear this remarkable sound come from this man who was the rather elderly Canon of the Bath Cathedral.

He continued chortling to himself as he dug deeper into the thought that had brought forth the laughter. Per usual, he was yet again thinking of a long ago event that particularly amused him.

It had occurred shortly after he was appointed to his current position. No one in Bath knew how difficult an opponent the good Canon could be.

The owner of the largest hotel in Bath had approached Donnell and, in a very grandiose tone, had assured him that they would be making their usual contribution to the church's coffers.

"No, my dear friend, I do believe it should be at least twice that amount. Now, should that bother you, I will have to inform our constabulary of the information I have just received. It seems that there are certain activities going on in your fine hotel that are not what I would call respectable."

The good man facing him turned explosively red and was about to scream out at this craven request, but his better notions prevented him from saying anything. He nodded and told the Canon that the money mentioned would be transferred to the Church's account that very afternoon.

Fact of the matter is that no such information had been given to Donnell. He had invented it that very moment. Here, some twenty five years after the event, this leader of the Church in Bath still enjoyed his ability to make things happen.

As long as there was no water pouring down on him, he would spend at least an hour each Saturday sitting in his tiny tree-sheltered garden which overlooked the wondrous grounds of the over half-mile long Royal Crescent.

He, like many, many thousands of others, had been astounded the first time he viewed the sights and indulged himself in the curative powers of the hot waters that gushed up from beneath the ground in a limitless supply.

That remarkable garden and the health-giving waters had brought fame and the dedication of visitors from all over the world.

All of this was just a part of what made Anthony Angus Donnell adore Bath. He had sworn, as a very young man to one day call this heavenly city his only home.

That pledge arrived hand and hand with a credo that he vowed to pursue when, in his early teens, he swore that he would succeed in everything he wanted to achieve. No one would be able to stop him. There was nothing that could stop him from fulfilling that vow.

The one outstanding physical presence in Bath was the Bath Cathedral which was affectionately called the Abbey by all locals of the city.

He was not to see the Cathedral until he was in his mid-twenties. His dreams about this wondrous structure were fulfilled with his first sight of her. Long famed for its beauty, she was as fine as anything he had ever viewed. That, and the city itself, convinced Anthony that he and Bath would become lifelong partners.

Having finally arriving in Bath, he worked harder and used every tactic, be it good or evil, to gain the pinnacle of success he had to achieve.

True to his initial dreams of success, Anthony had succeeded beyond his wildest dreams, for not only had he lived in Bath for many years, but he also had become a part of its hierarchy as the Canon of the Bath Cathedral.

The title, The Good Reverend, at the very least, bemused him, though he loved the ring of those words. He, more than anyone else, knew that there was not one thing about him that deserved to be labeled with the adjective 'good.'

Like everything else in his life, it had come to him as a result of his planning. Early in his career as a vicar, he had devoted much of his time to helping the least fortunate of his congregants and, at the same time, seeing to it that the wealthiest prospered even more because of the influence of his church.

The few quid he dispensed among the poor was but a pittance as compared to the vast sums that changed hands from all sorts of wealthy firms. Of course, he made certain that the church's finances would grow with each of his manipulations.

Rather quickly people began to talk about his being, 'Such a good man.' Some did so with true devotion while others did so with much scorn.

He had laughingly scoffed at the phrase and ended the thought with, "My goodness I would not be surprised if they soon will be calling me 'The Good Reverend.'"

It did not take too long for those words to become his unofficial title.

He equally loved the ring of his title, Canon Anthony Angus Donnell, as well as his sobriquet. Both titles made him a joyful of man.

He utilized this powerful post with a passion that was almost unique in the Church of England. He relished the opportunities he had to control the church's activities. Within his mind the Cathedral, and what it allowed him to do, coupled with the Gardens and the Waters of Bath, was a singular gift from God.

With that statement in his own mind, a question often arose, 'Whoever that might be?'

His friends would say he had been a beneficial force. His enemies would claim he was dictator of all that went on in Bath. In varying degrees both were correct. Those who opposed him paid heavily for that sin, and those that backed him went up a notch in church and civic affairs.

Yes, much of what he had done benefitted both the church and the city, but there was a segment of the population who swore he was a representative of the devil.

Though many years had passed since he first joined the ministry at Bath, he still considered himself as strong and as bright as he had ever been. Yes, on a rare occasion, he would wander into a room and then wonder what the devil he was doing there, but when serious matters arose, he could still rise to any challenge.

He had slowed his morning walks to the Cathedral quite a bit and, at times, just stayed at home for the day. However, let anyone dare to argue with him on some important issue and the Good Reverend would still leave his opponent much the worse for wear.

But this was Saturday afternoon, and, as usual, the Reverend sipped ever so slowly on his customary glass of sherry with not a care in the world.

He preferred the Sally Lunn Tea Biscuits over the smaller Bath buns that his elderly maid, Elizabeth, brought out, but either would do.

For many, many years his wife, Valerie, had cherished the ritual of bringing him the sherry and a choice of biscuits. But she had passed away some three years ago.

In all the years, no one, neither Valerie nor his four children, nor anyone else, had ever been asked to join the Reverend for a chat or to share a bit of sherry with him.

This was his hour to be alone. It had been so for some fifty years since he first started this sacred ritual, and he had never allowed anyone to share this pleasure with him.

From the very first, each Saturday had been filled with arduous decision making on how to approach the battles he was facing. Most importantly, they were always focused on the wars that he waged with himself on how he was going to advance his career and life style.

It had become a lifelong mission and one that he rarely failed at. By far, most had ended with him the victorious one. He delighted in each triumph. But now his major battles were over. He was at peace with himself and his need to stay competitive was over.

Today, he sat outside with a wry smile lightening the mask on his face. He realized that for some time now he no longer had anything to plan or plot for. There was no other position he wanted.

This past year, 1914, marked his sixty-fifth year, and he was much pleased with what he had done to achieve the status he now claimed.

Oh yes, there was still this minister to be reprimanded for so inadequately praising Duchess Winston for her latest contribution to the flower fund, or a dozen little chores that his staff had failed to perform to his liking.

He wasn't deeply concerned about any of the little wars he still waged to assure the advancement of some outwardly worthy cause. Only the ones that singularly advanced the reputation and stature of this wonderful churchman really interested him. It had been thus much of his life.

There had been some mighty scraps, and the strategy on how to handle each of them had been, for those fifty years, devised during his Saturday respite. Rarely did the implementation of the planning fail to succeed.

He had used every nefarious tool necessary to succeed. He did so with total disdain for those who cried foul at his tactics. If it meant lying or bribing or stealing, he accepted the need for those tactics.

Destroying an opponent brought particular pleasure to this holy man of God. To win each battle was all that mattered.

A sip of sherry, followed by a crunch of his cookie, and he was ready for the thoughts of the day. For whatever reason, this Saturday was filled with thoughts of his very early days and the life he lived that forced him to set goals and dream of a better life.

He was extremely proud of his achievements. His success proved that he was wiser and stronger than any of the weaklings he had beaten. He had few, if any, friends, but he had many supplicants who worshipped at his feet. They brought joy to this man who relished his self-given title of The Good Reverend.

Chapter Two

He had been born in the small city of Cork, Ireland, the youngest of seven children. Almost from the day of his birth, the entire family knew that he would be the tallest and best looking of the clan.

At the age of seven he was assigned the vital task of cleaning the filthy out-house that sat some feet behind the back of the hovel they lived in. Since he was the youngest, there was no one else to pass this honor to.

As soon as he could, he would verbalize his thoughts, as he told everyone that his name was not Tony, but Anthony, a name that he loved. Throughout his life he cut short anyone who called him anything but Anthony.

By the time he was just past seventeen, he was over six feet tall. He was an enormous lad. It must have been God who further blessed him with a warm smiling face that one and all conceded was the handsomest face in all of Cork.

Of greater import was the fact that he was also the brightest of his so crazed Irish family. It was his brain power that enabled his mother to get him enrolled in the one non-Catholic school in the town. There he consistently, when he decided to apply himself, was the brightest student they had ever enrolled in the school.

The early years of his life had been far from easy. Not that he was aware of it, but he was raised in the midst of the horrors brought on by the Irish Potato Famine. What passed for reality, and the way everybody he knew lived, was that he, like all of them, was always hungry.

Even as a thirteen year old, he wondered why the Irish seemed to be born for nothing but suffering while their overlords, the damned Englishmen, lived in a land of plenty. The words 'I hate the British,' was forever dropping out of his mouth, though he was never certain why he said it.

One Saturday afternoon, wonder of wonders, his father came home sober, but enraged. His furious animosity spewed forth with the vilest of words imaginable.

"Those bloody damned Englishmen were not content with just owning almost all of Ireland. They wanted to kill off anyone called Irish."

Anthony dared to ask his father why he hated the English with such a passion, and should he hate them too?

His father looked at his son and then, without a pause, smashed him in the face.

"You damned brat, you deserve a real beating for even thinking that the English were not the worst of beings ever created. Don't you ever forget that hating the Brits is the rule in this household."

He stormed away from Anthony and then spun back towards the boy, who immediately covered his face fearing another blow from his father. Instead his father continued the lecture.

"Listen close, you little shite, Lord John Russell, that eejit, who leads all of England, thinks we are the scum of the earth. Millions of us have already been killed off, but that isn't enough for him. He wants to kill all of us. Then he will really own every inch of our land. Not only do I want you to hate him, I want you to spend your whole life trying to kill him."

He punctuated his words with a right and a left smashing into Anthony's stomach.

"Because of what men such as Russell, John Peele and his fellow Whig Bastards have done to Ireland, you'll have good reason to hate them. Without them, this horror that goes on and on in Ireland could have been solved easily, but Russell preferred to sit on his fat ass and allow us Irishmen to either die or leave our land."

Of course, he didn't explain what Whig meant, and it sorely troubled Anthony as to what a wig had to do with so many of his classmates dying or moving away. He didn't have the courage to ask his father another question.

Much of what his father said went right past Anthony, but to this very day, the Reverend recalled exactly how his father's anti-British diatribe would end, and his reactions to those words and the passion that followed his hate-filled speech.

"They blame the potato blight for all the suffering we are having, but that is nonsense. It's all those English bastards who are getting as rich as can be by raping Ireland."

There wasn't one word uttered about how to beat the English and bring freedom to Ireland. Not a thought was expressed about how to chase 'those bastards' off their land. Only pure hatred gushed from his father's mouth.

They were still part of the United Kingdom of Great Britain and Ireland, but the disparity between how gloriously English people lived and the horror of life in Ireland was beyond belief.

Not only did it seem wrong to Anthony to merely curse out somebody, but not to do anything that could change the situation was an act of weakness that accepted failure.

His father's words echoed one constantly heard, as all in Southern Ireland's chorus kept screaming against the 'miserable bastards' who were devouring their land.

Anthony wholeheartedly derided their self-pity and acceptance of their horrid life. Yet, he hated the British for what they had done to Ireland, and he had equal disdain for the Irish who did nothing to win back their land.

Later he would change his tune. He would realize that the Irish were incapable of freeing themselves from the intolerable Brits. What became more evident to him was that being the victor was the only thing that mattered.

Maybe the English were miserably mean, maybe they were the worst people in the world, but they were victorious. All else meant nothing. They were winners now and forever. They would always triumph over the Irish who seemed to be born losers.

Hatred became the predominant force that drove Anthony Angus O'Donnell. This hatred was not just focused on the English. It was directed at everyone but himself.

This future minister of God thought not of God but of making everyone pay for this fury that constantly burned within him. Every day, yes, every day, this anger within him left no room for even an occasional giggle.

He despised his mother for her stupid acceptance of everything that was terrible, but the one who stirred the greatest anger was the man who was perpetually drunk. A man he loathed. No, it was far stronger than that. Even the word 'hated' minimized how deeply he detested his father.

From the first days he could walk on his own, he knew to stay away from this embittered man, whose only joy seemed to be the pleasure he got in beating anyone he happened upon in his house. A man who ruled everything in this dreadful hovel of a thing called their home

But it wasn't the beatings that he received from his dear father that drove Anthony crazy, it was the way his father, in particular, and the entire family treated his only sister.

Grace was one year older than Anthony and very slow. He was the sole member of the family that recognized how sweet and giving she was. Yes, she was far from bright.

But he could elicit a smile from her face that would glow with each tickle he gave her. She was the sole member of his family that loved him. Her constant plies, 'Anthony, I need a tickle' were instantly given and a smile would engulf her face and her giggles denoted total happiness.

Anthony loved to hear her sing with that miserable voice of hers. Everything she did was sweet and kind. Many an afternoon, he would sit with her and recite wild stories he would make up, and she would stare at him and say what wonderful adventures Anthony always had.

"You are my hero, Anthony. I wish I could go to school, so that I could be with you all the time."

She was his only joy. Somehow he would have to take her with him when he embarked on his real adventures.

Typical of his father's abuse of Grace were the nights his father would come home drunker than usual. His attempts to beat his wife or any of his children were easy enough to avoid, though he always managed to get in one strong slug at Grace, who was either playfully doing a jig in the corner or quietly singing to herself.

Anthony wanted to shout out to Grace and warn her to watch out, but he knew his father would then really go after her. Instead he stepped between the two.

This allowed Grace to hide behind her mother's skirt, while Anthony took a series of blows to every part of his body. That further infuriated Anthony. The only way he could defend the sibling he truly loved was to allow his father to vent his fury on his youngest son.

Most Irish boys affectionately called their fathers 'da.' That pleasant word never passed through Anthony's lips. He honored his father by simply despising the man.

Of course there was reason for how the man had turned out. Everything in his life was black. Both his parents had died when he was in his teens. He had gone from orphanage to orphanage until he was old enough to be thrown into the streets.

Early in his life he had shown strong signs of intelligence. He obtained a job of some stature, and proved quite adept at handling the work. He married and started raising a family.

All was well until the force of the Gorta Mor, the Irish Famine, struck.

Over a million people would eventually leave Ireland, and over a million Irish people would die. He was not that fortunate. The job he loved was taken over by an Englishman, and he spent many years without work until he stumbled upon a job sweeping up the debris in a local boat yard.

Needless to say, his income was but slightly over a pittance.

Though he was physically bigger than most on the job, he was always the loser and rarely the winner in any fight. He found his first victories when each of his children came along. Be they male or female, he could whip the hell out of them. Add some liquor to the encounters, and he became a hero in his own eyes.

He kept spewing forth loud and constant verbal attacks on his mortal enemies, the British.

To Anthony, that was garbage. The British were the winners, and the Irish would always be the worst of losers.

His older brothers, sensing Anthony's ever growing hatred for their father, tried to reason with their youngest brother.

"You know he wasn't always as crazy as he is now. He had a good job as a clerk in a fine office, but that disappeared. Luckily he got the one he now has so we have some money coming in. He hates his work. So he drinks and has become the crazy man you know. Stop acting a maggot and give him a little room."

Anthony's retort was, "When he sobers up, I will try to like him. Til then, I will always hate that bastard."

Like the rest of his family, Anthony learned early on to steer clear of that man. One joy he could always achieve was getting out of bed as early as possible. He would then try to steal something to eat and rush away from the chance of meeting with that ogre. Let him find someone else to beat.

He would fly out of this house that reeked of the vilest of odors imaginable. There was nothing in that dreadful place or, for that matter, in his entire life that gave him a moment of true pleasure. Simply stated, he, like every Irishman, spent every day fighting to merely stay alive.

Their house was no different from most of the other Irish edifices that clung to the hills around Cork. There was no indoor toilet. The windows were a glassless hole in the four walls. The floors were all dirt filled and not honored with a single piece of wood. Its largest room was the kitchen with the tiniest of sinks, running water which was off far more than on, and a forever shaking table with half broken chairs around it.

There were several beds scattered through the rooms. The youngest learned that they were expected to sleep on any part of the always damp floor that they fell upon.

But they clung to this mansion with a passion, because it came with a small potato patch attached to the property. They were proud of this possession, for it was one of the largest patches in all of Cork. Like most similar patches in Ireland, it was the source of most of their food, necessary to feed them for an entire year.

It did so until, like all the other sources of food in this stricken land, it hardly issued anything edible.

Ireland's lack of money meant no lessening of the rent for the privilege of living in their hovel. Not paying the rent could result in instant eviction. Anthony's father, no matter what his condition, never forgot to put aside the money for that pay date. There was only one answer to the horrors that surrounded the boy. As soon as feasible, he would become a proper English gentleman.

Chapter Three

One could perhaps understand his father's way of life. Just facing each onerous day was, at best, a loathsome burden. But there were millions of other Irishmen suffering as badly as Anthony's father who remained decent people. Only his extremity of ego and devouring rancor forced their father to be the vilest, most hate-filled man in all of Cork. Said man, at his best, was not the easiest of Irishmen.

Liquor provided the backbone for his father and most of the other Irish men. But he was one of the fortunate ones. He had a job. The average age for the men of this pitiful nation to die was just shy of forty- two.

The company he worked for was, of course, English owned. It built small boats that were put to use all over the world. His vitally important duties consisted entirely of going through the shipyard from morning to night cleaning debris from the path of the real workers. He also knew that there were thousands of other Irishmen who would kill to get his job.

Saturday, the men collected their meager weekly salary as they left the yard, which closed promptly at six.

Just across from his work site was a small pub which welcomed Anthony's father. He would race to the pub, drink down as much as they would let him. Promptly at seven o'clock, he would get too boisterous, and the pub owners would have him thrown out.

It was the only day of the week he could afford the pub. By Wednesday he would have run out of funds to buy even a small bottle of lager or, in really dire times, he would purchase some dreadful 'poteen,' a home brew made by a friend of his. He was at his meanest on days when even that was unavailable and he was stone sober.

Those were the days that his entire family tried its hardest to hide from their 'loving' father.

Anthony found that he desperately needed a period of time away from his family and away from his father. The problems he faced were so massive that it required a place that would allow him the freedom to just think of the means to escape the tortures he endured each day.

The grin on the good Canon's face grew as he thought about his unfortunately choosing for his first haven what would turn out to be a seriously leaky rowboat that necessitated more bailing than he wanted.

It all came vividly back to him. He was not quite seventeen, and the problems of the moment had taken over his soul. Of course, it was his miserable father who, unwittingly, would put him into that boat on that dire day so many, many years ago. That long gone Saturday turned into an epic event for the boy.

Most days, particularly Saturday, the family would go on 'father alert.' The lack of liquor built a ring storm within the man.

The family knew about what time the man would come stumbling home and be prepared for the onslaught.

He would grumble his way into the tiny house. The first of his many children he came upon would be the unlucky victim of a merciless thrashing.

The previous day Anthony had managed to avoid any sight of his father, but he was not that lucky on this Saturday.

Normally his drunken father was easy to avoid, but on this day he was cold sober. It was obvious that a fire was burning within him and he was determined to extinguish those flames by severely beating the one who had caused him to almost explode with anger.

Anthony would soon find out what it meant to cause trouble to descend on his father.

It would not be the first time his father had beaten him, but it would be far and away the worst beating he ever received.

Unfortunately, Anthony was outside on all fours trying to dig up what looked like an edible potato. This patch was just fifty feet from his house. He was absorbed in his task when suddenly a hand grabbed him by the neck and dragged him to his feet.

Whoever it was that lifted him up then hit him in the face with a bag that had something very heavy in it. Anthony then felt himself being thrown through the front door of his house. By then he realized that it was his father who was trying to kill him.

"Now you efffin and blinkin piece of garbage you'll be payin for all I had to take this day."

Fortunately, his father was so feverish in his desire to beat Anthony that he missed many of his more lethal shots to the head or stomach of his youngest child. But the blows that landed went a long way to increase the hatred Anthony bore for his father and the need to flee from this horrid family of his.

Whatever hell his father was spewing out made little sense, but Anthony could see pure fury pouring from this beast of a man.

"You rotten little bum. Do you know where I spent this afternoon?"

He then stopped talking and managed to get in two real zingers to the head and back of Anthony.

"No, it wasn't at the pub. No, no, no. This morning at my job I get a note from a thing they call a teacher. It says that he hopes I can spare some time after work today to meet with him in his office at the school so we might discuss something of importance. Right away I know he is going to tell me how smart you are. So I skip the pub and go to the man's office."

The man's face is a complete opposite from the nice words he is saying.

"I decided to get there real early so I can hear the good news about you and then celebrate in fine fashion. I lie to my boss and tell him I am terrible sick and could I leave work a little early. He says okay."

Anthony is lying on the floor not knowing how to avoid the next blows that are certain to come pouring down upon him,

"And that was no lie I told him. Me sickness is having to go to that school and have that snot-nosed English teacher of yours yelling at me about what a miserable one you are."

Another smash to Anthony's head sent him reeling face down on the floor.

"So there I was and, yes, he starts out by saying that I could address him as Mr. Blake. Mr. Blake, sir. Right off I know this is not going to be a good meeting, and why the hell do I want to spend any time with this puffer, this roaring molly of a man."

All the while he is talking, he is holding Anthony by one hand and bashing him with the other. This huge figure of a man drags his son into the kitchen, while mother and everyone else that was home wisely moved as far away as possible from the fracas.

"He starts off for a few minutes telling me what a smart kid you are. Your dear Mr. Puffer Blake then goes on to blaming me for your being such a scoundrel, such a waste of time. I am the cause for everything bad about you, and if I don't shape up and put you on the right path, your days at the school are all but over."

Again a bit of a slugfest launched at Anthony.

"And then he goes off on another god-awful tearing you apart. But all of sudden I don't know what in the hell he is talking about. Then the pissing rat goes off into what changed his life. It seems there is someone named Jane Austen who is the wonder of wonders. How the hell am I supposed to know who the hell Jane Austen is, and what in the name of all that is holy has she got to do with this beating he is laying on me?"

The fury seemed to ebb for a moment.

"He nicely asked me if I had read anything by Jane Austen. So, thinking it would make him easier on me, I said something like, 'Hasn't everyone?'"

The Good Reverend recalls this crazed man then jumping up in the air and shouting right into my face "Of course they haven't, because they are all stupid ignoramuses like yourself."

Another look at his son brought the task at hand. The anger exploded in his father and Anthony caught an enormously hard shot to his stomach.

"Have I told you that he is seated high in his chair while I am standing humbly in front of him with me hat in me hands, and I don't get in a word other than 'no, sir,' or 'yes, sir.' And he keeps kicking the shite out of me and killing me with the bollocks about you. Then off he storms again about Jane Austen."

His father quieted and seemed to be reflecting on what Blake had made him endure.

What was most puzzling to Anthony, was how that tiny mouse of a man, Mr. Blake, had been, 'beating the shite out of his father.' Not a chance in hell.

A brief pause and then the voice screamed out even louder.

"Is you listening to me? Here I am working myself to the bone in that damned shipyard. I am knockered out every day of me life and getting paid practically nothing. I kin hardly keep this family going, yet your Mum and me are saving every penny we can so that we can keep our wonderful bairn, that means you, you worthless king of garbage, in that school. Well let me tell you something, you little weasel, it be time for us to make some changes here."

At this point, the good Mr. O'Donnell planted his huge foot on the boy's chest.

"You are the youngest of our brood and, without a doubt, the worst. Every one of your brothers and sisters are just fine. But you don't deserve to be a part of this family."

His father walked away for a second and then launched another kick into Anthony all the while screaming out at a very frightened young Anthony.

"Di ya... I say di ya ken what that perfumed wiss told me?"

His father's rage took over his ability to talk. It grew exponentially as he just kept punching the air as if he was beating someone.

"I am standing there while he is beating at me like 'tis all me fault. He says you are one of the brightest kids he has, but you have never been taught proper manners, and you couldn't give a damn about anything but causing trouble. And I'm there like some dumb fool of a man just taking it all in. Then he flat out screams at me that you and your stupid ways better get to changing, or your ass is going to be thrown the hell out of that school."

Once again his father seemed to quiet down, but this made Anthony even more frightened, because he didn't know what the next explosion would bring down on him.

"Well, this Irishman is sure as hell never again going to take that garbage from anyone, anyone. So listen up real good."

He leaned close to his son's right ear and, as he spoke the following real low, the spit from his anger spilled all over Anthony.

"I can still smell that girly perfume he is wearing, and it really stinks. He is practically on top of me whispering that you can and must change your ways, or you will be gone from that school forever."

In total fury, he grabbed his son by both arms and plucked him off the floor and forced him upright, face against the wall. With one hand he took the boy's neck and slowly began to squeeze. With the other hand he kept thrusting the heavy bag into his son's face.

"Di you know what is in this bag? No? Well let me tell you. It is a gift from that plum fairy. It is every book that Austen woman has written, and he expects you to read every word in them and write him a report on all those damned books."

Books were easy. Why was his father making such a to-do about doing some reading?

"From this day forward you are going to suck up to Blake and do anything that has to be done to get to stay in that school. If he wants you to read every book in this town you are going to jump to it. Keep reminding yourself that if you ain't in school you ain't in this house either. So, here is what we will be doing from now on."

The forthcoming plan, of course, had really been outlined by Mr. Blake, who had pointed out, 'Just being bright is not good enough to keep him in our school. There must be drastic changes in that boy of yours.'

Ever so slowly the pressure increased on his son's throat.

"Di you hear me you little runt? That pissant of a teacher is never going to lecture me ever again. If he goes after me like he did today, I will beat him to a pulp, and then I will kill you."

Another tightening of the massive hand left very little room for air to pass through.

"So, the choice is yours. Start sucking up right now to that bum and do whatever he wants you to do. I am telling you to do whatever you can to get him to like you. And, if you don't do it quickly, you'll never be seeing your eighteenth birthday."

Another smash to the face, and an increase of the pressure on Anthony's throat caused him to almost stop breathing. Then, with a final kick, he dropped Anthony to the floor and walked off.

Anthony kept inhaling as much air as he could force down his throat.

The anger that boiled within him was not directed at his father but at himself. The vow he had sworn to uphold came rushing back to him. He would kill that man before he ever had to take another beating. And he would soon be leaving this house, and that meant as quickly as feasible.

He must find a place to think, to plan, to put into action what must be done as quickly as possible. And, he must start this very moment.

The waters off the coast of Cork seemed to be the ideal place to be alone and to dream.

Chapter Four

The good Reverend vividly recalled his screaming out to himself on that dreadful day.

Essentially it was, 'You phony bastard, if you ever again go to hit me, it will be you who will become the dead man. Neither you or that teacher or anybody else is going to stop me from being someone important in this world.'

Dear father had read Blake correctly. All the kids knew that Blake was one of those funny men. Blake was in his early thirty's and therefore the youngest teacher in the school. The Head Master at the school was delighted that a man of his educational qualifications, and a graduate of Oxford, would come to Cork to teach at such a humble school.

When questioned about why he had come to Ireland, he would respond that he felt the opportunities that were open there were of a superb nature.

Actually, he had been fired from a lower school in his home town of Manchester, England, for sexual misdemeanors. He fled to Ireland to rebuild his life.

And that would be the tool to be used to steer Blake into doing whatever Anthony wanted him to do. Anthony planned to twist and turn Blake till the man was crazed with expectations. Then, at the proper moment, he was going to be used and used and used until he handed Anthony his passport out of Ireland.

Anthony thought that the first thing he was going to do this Monday was to go to school and start wooing that little weasel. He would tell Blake that all he was interested in was remaining in school and becoming the best one in the class. Then he would thank him for the loan of those Jane Austen books, whoever the hell she is.

For several hours he rehearsed a speech he would give to Mr. Poof. He twisted and turned each word he would utter until he felt totally confident it would achieve the result he wanted.

He finally settled with, 'I apologize for being such a stupid young imbecile. I desperately need someone like you to help me to learn all I need to know. I realize I have to change my ways and follow someone like you.'

Hopefully, Blake would help him through his current schooling and then help him flee to college. And, if that help wasn't forthcoming, he would just run away from this sick family and dreadful town.

Anthony equally cursed his father and Mr. Blake and everyone else who made his life so terrible. What had just happened would never happen again. The next time his father came at him he would find a boy who was stronger, faster and angry enough to beat the hell out of him.

He would command everything about his life. Idiots like his teacher and his father would one day be sucking up to him. He would use them, and they wouldn't even know that they were being used.

The boy indeed was very smart. He had no real friends, and knew that if he was going to change his life, it had to start now. He must declare war against the world and, to do so, he had only himself to rely upon.

He knew that his father had taught him one important lesson. He would never become a drunken, worthless Irish bum like his father. He thanked his father for the physical stature he had inherited, and vowed that if forced to, he would use his strength to kill the man.

There was no question in his mind but that poof of a teacher would soon be doing everything he could to win Anthony's favor.

He was going to be a success. Yes, that's right, a big success.

He would change everything in his life, even though he had no money, no strength over others, no secret powers that would make others bow to his wishes.

Chapter Five

Later that Saturday afternoon, he found the perfect place to be alone to think about the wars he was about to launch. He found a little row boat drifting just off the harbor. Albeit being a damned leaky rowboat, he would hold his first conference with himself quietly out at sea. There he would determine how to handle this battle to change what he was that day.

From that day on his favored activity was to race down to the docks, steal a rowboat, and spend the next few hours dreaming of what his future would be. It would become a weekly habit.

Anthony was always cautious to steal better boats for his weekly debate with himself. He would row fiercely away from the harbor-- his mind focused on how he could best use his dear teacher, his family and his stupid friends. Everybody he knew, and the others he would get to know were to be tools he would use in his oncoming battles.

That two hour conference would be the first of almost fifty years of plotting the road to success. That first self-debate would grow and become crucially important to him and reconvene every week for the remainder of his life.

His supple mind, and his willingness to do anything were the linchpins to win the battles ahead. He would lie, cheat, steal or do any vile act that was necessary to emerge as the success he dreamed he must be. That mantra would be repeated every day of his life.

He laughed at the thought of his father and his teacher and all the others he would be using in the years to come. They, and everyone else in his life, would be mere tools in the great battle he was planning.

'If that makes me some miserable human being, I don't care. I am going to get everybody to think I am the best man in the world, while all I'll be thinking of will be how I have to use them to push me ahead. Being a success, a big success, is all that matters.'

Somehow, he would wage this great battle to triumph over everyone.

Chapter Six

Reverend Donnell recalled that Saturday so long ago was also a perfect Cork spring day, and, the use of the boat delighted him.

He smiled as he envisioned himself, some three days later, telling three of his classmates about the great fun one could have by tearing off on a great adventure on the waters off Cork.

This day he had introduced his friends to the joys they could have by stealing a boat and become Admirals of the sea for a few hours.

For the longest period of time it had been just three, Patrick Daly, and Timothy O'Rourke who, with Anthony as their leader, had terrorized the area, but they had just added Martin Flarity to the group.

He was a bit younger and frightened silly at all times, but they needed a 'good little guy' to counterbalance their reputation, and he, despite his fears, gloried in being one of this batch of, in his eyes, heroes

Anthony and his gang would as often as feasible steal a rowboat and spend a few hours of wondrous fishing or just sailing from beach to beach.

One day the four boys were having a jolly old time when they selected the right vehicle for their seaside adventure.

They steered here and there and then headed out around a jetty that extended quite a bit into the sea. Laughingly, they steered around the corner and almost ran dead on to an English patrol boat. They were quickly hauled up on the vessel.

Need we say that all four lads were terrified and that word was a gross understatement of their feelings.

Poor Martin Flarity, on his first step up the ladder to the English vessel, clearly wet himself. The tears flowing down his face covered the fact that he could not speak a word.

"All right you little Irish bastards, who is the genius among you who came up with the idea to hijack that boat?"

This roared from the fierce-looking captain of the River Boat.

Instantly, Anthony, followed by the other two, pointed at the now numb Martin. It was obviously such an utter piece of fiction that all of the English sailors broke into a storm of hysterical laughter.

When they recovered, the captain gave the boys a five minute frightening talk about what they could do to this riff-raff before them. The captain then took each of the boys and, one by one, threw them into the sea.

As he grabbed Martin, the last of the group, he yelled to his crew, "What should it be, throw him out now before he stinks up our boat, or should we give him a solid old whipping?"

A unanimous cry to let the fish feast on him resulted in him sailing some twenty feet through the air before he hit the water. Somehow, the boys managed, despite the soaking, to swim to the shore.

The good Canon erupted into hearty laughter as he recalled thinking of those friends and wondered what had happened to Martin. Without a doubt that poor, always frightened little boy, must have grown up to be the arch-typical loud mouthed, but frightened little Irishman.

Chapter Seven

During his, as he called them, life-saving sessions, he, of course, felt total disdain for his almost always drunken father, but he felt equal despair for his mother. She devoted far more time to her husband and the ridiculous little church she worshipped at than to him or any of her other children.

When he thought of his mother, he was always deeply puzzled. Though worn to a frazzle, she still showed signs of an early beauty. At times she let out a delicious laugh and a smile that could bring happiness to all those around her. In their private conversations, she spoke intelligently and with a genuine sweetness. Yet, she had one great flaw. She tolerated that monster of a husband far more than anything else in her life.

Other than Grace, he could not care less for his siblings, as they hardly knew he existed. It seemed as if the entire world was conspiring to make his life a total misery.

On his first outing with his 'boat de jour,' the fury he carried within him put powerful force into each stroke of the oars, and the boat was rapidly propelled onwards.

And with each such stroke he would cry out, "I hate them all, and I'm not going to let them stop me from being me."

Bit by bit, he got far enough out of sight of land, and when he could barely see the mainland, he dropped his oars and just let the boat drift here and there. Without a thought, he kept bailing away while his mind tested the waters of much greater matters.

He was thoroughly bewildered by how stupid each of his brothers and his sweet sister were. How could he be so different from them?

What bothered him most was that they all seemed perfectly happy being part of the horror called the O'Donnell family. He prayed that his mother had some torrid romance, and he was fathered by a man of intelligence and great esteem and not the drunken buffoon who now played the father role.

Could it be that she really cared for that man or was it her total immersion, as a believing Catholic, that carried her through each day and mandated her total allegiance to that vile man?

She had probably told her youngest son a million times that God and Jesus were with him every moment of every day, and Anthony would wonder where the hell were those two when her husband was beating the holy shit out of him.

The fact that she remained that man's devoted wife, and she had not left him or killed him, made Anthony question her sanity.

What disturbed him most was the knowledge that dominated his life. If he stayed where he was for much longer, he would heed the advice he wanted to give his mother. He would kill that son-of-a-bitch.

That certainty forced his conversation with his alter-ego to dwell on what he must do to save himself. Slowly the idea arose that he had to set some overall goals that would free him from the torture of staying where he was.

He quickly knew that to maintain any sense of self preservation, he must get out of his current environs. It was obvious and, as soon as possible, that must be accomplished.

Some of his older brothers were not too bad, but look at them. There wasn't a one that wouldn't, sure as hell, follow the path set by their father. Definitively, this was not for Anthony Angus O'Donnell.

But he did not have the other side of the coin. The far more difficult assignment which would determine what he had to do to allow him to fly away from this horror he now lived in.

So his number one priority was to get the hell away from that world as fast as he could.

"How do I do that?"

He needed a tool that was attainable and could put him on a track to success. Slowly one word emerged. Education! Yes, education. Education could be the tool that could cut him loose from the chains that labeled him an 'O'Donnell.'

Okay, he was smart enough to get good marks. That was easy. But with no money to pay for his schooling, he could not settle for just those good marks. He had to get the very best ones possible. He must stand out as a student so bright that colleges would be fighting to get him into their school. Yes, that is what he will need if he was to attend the best school in Ireland, Trinity College in Dublin.

And then it struck him. Mr. Blake, the great big molly, would be the key to all that Anthony needed

"Mr. Blake, sir, I want to introduce you to your new best friend. Me. That is right, sir. And you are going to be my best friend. And I want to thank you in advance for assuring that I receive the perfect grades that are going to bring me to Trinity College. You may ask why I am so sure of what I say. It is because I know the way to get you so excited that you will be panting to do everything I say."

Once Blake was brought into the fold, it would be an easy leap for his new dear friend to become the prime advocate to deliver what Anthony wanted. That delivery promised the perfect path for the young man to escape being just another O'Donnell.

On the coming Monday, upon entering the school, he went directly to the office of Mr. Blake.

"Yes, Anthony, what is it you want?"

"Sir, I just want to apologize for the way I have behaved before now. I have been a terrible kid, and that is wrong, and I intend to change from that."

He finished his little speech with the sentence that he had spent much time on.

"I want you to know that I will do anything that will make you happy with me."

With a bit of tremor in his voice those words were more than rewarded when Mr. Blake's frown seemed to change almost into a small smile, though all he said was, "We shall see, we shall see."

Chapter Eight

The following day Anthony was leaving for home when he spied Mr. Blake standing at the school's front door. He approached his teacher and very humbly asked if he could have a word with him.

"Of course, what is it?"

"Well, sir, I first want to thank you for the books you have loaned me. I really want to come up with a great report, but I am beginning to be confused with 'Sense and Sensibility.' It is getting very puzzling to me as it nears the end. Would it be possible that you can help me with it?"

Blake just stared at Anthony and then slowly said, "Well, I have much to do at home but, why don't you come by my house an hour or two from now, and I'll be able to spare some time then. Do you know where I live?"

"Oh, yes I do, sir. And I really appreciate your giving me the time. I am looking forward to working with you."

A big smile of gratitude graced his face and off he ran. Blake kept his eye on the boy as he sped away.

Promptly at four P.M., Anthony knocked at Blake's front door and hardly a second went by before it opened, and he was greeted by a very casually dressed Blake.

"Well, you certainly are on time. Come in."

This house, though small, was a castle in comparison to Anthony's shack. It was furnished perfectly and had a sense of being kept clean and polished at all times.

"Follow me to my study. That is where I do all my work."

If the remainder of the house was nice, the study was glorious. There was picture after picture lining the walls, each of which bore the resemblance of some great male warrior reaching high with a saber or standing tall atop a strong stallion.

"Oh my gosh, look at all those great pictures on the wall. They sure look like fine gentlemen."

"Do you like them, Anthony?"

"Yes sir. They all look like heroes. One day I am going to be a hero too."

"I am sure you will. Tell me something, do you like men?"

"Well, that's a difficult question. I don't like men who can't even speak nicely. I hate the men who don't know how to dress. And I really detest the men who seem to be drunk all the time and, like my father, seem to enjoy beating on people weaker than them. When I get older, I will never do that. Some day, I am going to buy fancy shirts and good shoes and a lot of things that make me happy. I guess I mean I am going to try and dress as nicely as you do."

"Thank you for the compliment."

"No, sir, I really should be thanking you so much for waking me up to what I really want."

"Don't be silly. Now let's get down to work. What are the questions that Jane Austen has posed for you?"

Anthony had prepared for that question. He handed Mr. Blake a piece of paper on which he had written some twenty different sentences.

"The only book I have read so far is 'Sense and Sensibility' and that took me a ton of time. Of that list of questions I gave you, there are four that really puzzle me."

The true fact is that Anthony had only skimmed through the book in order to find good questions to ask.

"Well, I presume the first question is the hardest one, eh? Do tell me what that is."

"Well, I am a little embarrassed, but I can't come up with any idea about what the title means. I've tried very hard, but I just don't understand what 'Sense and Sensibility' means."

Blake broke out into a fit of laughter. It took him many moments to calm down.

The scene came back to the Reverend as crystal clear as if it had just occurred. He remembered Mr. Blake as being very short and a far from good looking man, and, when he laughed, he exposed an absolutely dreadful set of teeth that only served to emphasize his ugliness. The Reverend recalled how difficult it was for him to keep a straight face when Blake exposed those teeth.

Anthony recovered by saying, "Mr. Blake, I don't like being laughed at because I don't know something. That isn't fair."

"No, no, Anthony, I am not laughing at you. I am laughing with you. You see most people do not understand the title. And, I am not certain if Miss Austen did."

Blake then opened the sheet and, after reading all the questions, commended Anthony.

"Anthony, these remarks show some very good thinking. There is a brain in that handsome face of yours. We will both be learning much in these sessions together."

"Does that mean that we will be doing this again?"

"Would that make you happy?"

"I think happy is not a strong enough word to tell you how good I would feel."

"Well, let's see how things go on. We can discuss that later this evening. Now, why don't we get into your questions?"

"Mr. Blake, may I first ask a question that does not come from the book?"

Blake nodded his approval and Anthony proceeded.

"In one of the books there was a brief biography of Miss Austen that said she really was of very modest means, but she had fallen in love with Bath, England, and that she had spent a good deal of her life there. Is it true that Bath is one of the great cities of England?"

"That really requires three answers. Yes, she did spend a good part of her life in Bath. But, the truth of it is that she had a roaring hatred for the city. It was her parents who adored Bath and kept her there despite her feelings about the city. And is Bath a wonder? It is as close to perfection as any city can be. I have been there but once and fell in love with it. I would be eternally grateful if I could spend the rest of my days in that marvelous little village."

Anthony's reply was muted and equally strange.

"Well, I hope your get there and, maybe someday I will be able to visit you there."

The two just stared at one another for a short period and then Blake brought them back into focus.

"I find your questions to be very interesting. However, most of them can only be answered by Miss Austen herself. Unfortunately, she died many years ago. Possibly we will find answers to some of them."

"How do we do that?"

"There is an author's device that I believe handles the questions quite well. As I see it, the first question is the title itself, then the family moving from house to house so frequently, followed by the three Dashwood sisters clinging so tightly to each other, and, finally, Marianne Dashwood dashing off to marry, as you call him, that Brandon chap. Have I posed the questions correctly?"

Anthony, with mouth agape, merely nodded his assent.

"Well, the answer is the same for all four questions. What Miss Austen has done is lure the reader into making decisions that then bring said reader into deeper thoughts of the book. Unfortunately, her works initially led to almost total dislike for the book when they were first issued. It really wasn't until after her death that the popularity of her works emerged. Or should we say that the readers had become more sophisticated."

"Do you think the people who didn't like her books were bothered by the same questions that I stumbled over?"

"I am not certain, but just as you were not ready for her work, I am inclined to believe that they were put into the very same position."

"Mr. Blake, you have just made me very happy."

Blake was delighted with how the evening was going. There was no doubt that he had found a unique boy. One who was not only bright but obviously accessible. This boy must be handled carefully.

It took almost two hours to go through each of the questions, as Blake posed different possible answers for each question. He and Anthony would discuss each idea he brought forth and then decide which answer was the most appropriate. He was continually impressed with Anthony's nimble brain.

"My goodness, I have let the time fly by, Anthony, but I have much enjoyed the intellect you have displayed."

"I don't know how to say this, Mr. Blake, but I have never enjoyed myself so much as I have done being with you. So I thank you so much."

"Well, we both have had a grand time. I tell you what, why don't we try this again some other evening? We could discuss school matters or anything else that perks our interest. Does that interest you at all?"

"Interest me? I think I don't believe you really are willing to do so. Yes, yes. I would love to meet with you as often as you would like. And, Mr. Blake, to me you are as much a hero as any one of the men on your walls."

Blake laughingly claimed that those words constituted a huge overstatement but, nevertheless, thanked Anthony for the compliment.

"Well, let us see if we can keep this up at a very high level. Why don't you drop by the same time this Friday? If things work out well, we could plan on every Monday and Friday. What do you feel about that?"

"I feel like I am the luckiest kid in Ireland."

Blake then led his young friend towards the front door. It was then that Anthony realized that not once had Blake so much as touched him or even shook his hand. They had never been closer than several feet apart. Blake had handled himself perfectly.

"Mr. Blake. Can I ask you one more question?"

"Ask away."

"You are the smartest man I have ever met. Yet here you are, an Englishman, teaching in this dinky school. Why?"

Blake stared at the boy. Hs eyes almost started to tear up but he regained his composure.

"Anthony, you have done nothing but compliment me all evening. That question requires a good deal of time to answer and one day I will. Until then, just accept the fact that I am a little different than most. But, do know that these meetings with you will be as rewarding for me as I hope they will be for you."

And Anthony thought, *'Well played Mr. Blake. We will see this Friday who is the smarter in moving this game along.'*

Chapter Nine

The good Reverend, though half asleep, chuckled to himself. This pursuit of his early years was such a pleasure. Dear Mr. Blake had been such a simpleton. The Reverend recalled how bored he was at that second meeting which had followed the exact same track as the first meeting. Was it the third or the fourth meeting that Blake had made the first obvious sexual approach?

No, it definitely was not the third meeting. He recalled that Anthony had not even knocked on the door before it sprung open revealing Mr. Blake, smilingly, welcoming Anthony into the house.

"Hello, Anthony. It is so nice to see you here. Once again, you are so prompt. I was looking out my study window and saw you coming up the path, so I saved you the trouble of knocking."

Of course Anthony thought, 'He was probably painfully waiting for me to appear. Me thinks his appetite for me is growing faster than his caution.

As was by now customary, they sauntered off towards the studio and, for the first time, Blake gently placed his arm around the boy's shoulder.

"You know, Anthony, we are getting along so well that I am going to allow you a special privilege. My full name is

Stephen Culver Blake and I would like you to call me Steve whenever we are alone, like now. But, you must never call me anything but Mr. Blake in school. Do you agree to that?"

"Oh that is great. And it will be our secret. I love secrets."

"Good. Then let's shake hands on that."

The two hands were clasped and Anthony instantly thought, 'That's a bit long for a simple handshake isn't it Stevie, Weevie?'

In the telling of his first name Blake also had taken the opportunity for the first time to, oh so carefully, fondle the boy. At first it was just a longer pat of the knee than necessary and then a real squeeze of the thigh. This was followed by a very soft caress of Anthony's face. All of this, without any comment from either party.

And each of his teacher's moves were greeted with an adoring smile from the boy.

Finally, Anthony thought, 'With every one of those sweet little moves, my dear Mr. Blake, you are a step closer to putting me into Trinity College.'

This was the perfect time to plunge yet another dagger into dearest Stevie.

"Mr. Blake, no I mean, Steve. May I ask you something that is very important to me?"

"Aren't we Steve and Anthony? And doesn't that mean we are good friends, and, doesn't being good friends mean we can ask anything of one another?"

"Yes, you are right, but I am embarrassed with what I want to say, but here goes."

Anthony swallowed, took in too much air and seemed to choke. It was a marvelous performance on his part.

"I am sorry, but here I go."

Another long pause and finally the words crept out of his mouth.

"I don't want to grow up and be like my father or my oldest brothers. All they do is curse and get drunk and beat everyone smaller than they are. I hate my father. I don't want to grow up and become another drunken O'Donnell. Steve, was your father like my father?"

"Oh no, Anthony, he was at all times as sober as a judge. He ruled over everything with a very strict hand. My father only used words to dominate the family. But I tell you that he hurt me far more than your drunken father could even think of hurting you."

"I don't understand that."

"Anthony, my father is a very successful business man. My two older brothers are even more successful in business than he is. And then I came along. There is nothing about me that he likes."

"But how could he hurt you?"

"I was once caught at doing something that the world considers sinful. I was happily teaching at a small college at the time. When father heard what I had done, he arranged for this position in Cork and shipped me out here with the specific instructions that I could never return to England. So, I guess, I have as much reason to hate my father as you do yours."

"There is nothing you could have done that is bad. You are my idol. I want to be just like you. I want you to teach me to speak like you and to act like you and dress like you. I guess I want you to teach me to be you."

"Why that is the nicest compliment I have ever had, and I thank you for it. I promise you I have been much pleased with you, and I have given much thought to how much I can offer you."

He then gave Anthony the slightest brush of a kiss on his cheek and stepped back.

"How one lives one's life is of singular importance. But the best way I can help you is by being myself and let you absorb what you can. I would hope you can fit into my style of life. The answer of who you want to be will be your decision. Hopefully, you will enjoy the way I live. All I am certain of is that we will both have much pleasure as our relationship develops."

"Steve, you are wonderful and, of course, I'll do whatever you say."

"Well, what I say is let's have some tea and cookies. I want you to know that I made these cookies myself. I am a very fine chef so, possibly some evening you can get to stay for dinner and maybe spend the night here."

"That sounds so great. I could tell my folks that a smart kid from school and I are working on a project for our history class and we need a night to finish it. I know my folks would go for that."

Blake lit up like a Guy Fawkes blazer.

"That would make me very happy. And I could teach you some things that might make you very happy."

He then, for the first time, hugged Anthony. The embrace was tender and non-threatening. He then backed away and went to the tea service.

"Let's celebrate with a cup of tea and some of my special cookies and then we will get back to Miss Austen."

The Reverend recalled that in the remainder of that afternoon Blake, some three or four times, would allow himself the joy of placing his hand on Anthony's shoulder. Twice a gentle squeeze of his knee was a seemingly innocent response from Blake to a particularly bright remark from Anthony. Each touch was greeted with a warm smile from Anthony.

It ended at that. Nothing went further than man and boy enjoying the companionship of each other.

Truth be told, it was for both Blake and Anthony as fitting a two hour period as could have been. Both were very satisfied with what transpired.

It was not too long before Anthony realized that Blake was not planning on anything other than another feel or two that might promote their romance. The thought that maybe he would have to be a bit more aggressive did enter his mind, but Anthony decided that slower was better than too fast and he would see what occurred on their next meeting.

He was certain that good old Stevie could not restrain himself much longer than that. How he would handle the situation was clear in his mind. Mr. Blake had to be the one who pushed their relationship onto the next level. If nothing eventful occurred on Friday he would still leave Blake panting away for him. When he got Blake even more aflame, he would go in for the kill and be on his way to Trinity.

Time was on Anthony's side and, strangely enough, he was not at all worried about how it would proceed. He was totally in command of the progress he and Blake were making.

Jane Austen and her books were the main topic of conversation and they both felt they knew her better. They agreed that she was a remarkable writer.

It was Anthony who took them both down another route when he mentioned how glad he was that she didn't write that smutty stuff where a man and a women do all those horrid things to one another. And then he added, "I like to read stuff when men enjoy each other. That seems like fun."

Blake was sorely tempted to pursue that opening but backed away. Instead he asked Anthony how he got to read that kind of material.

"Oh, there are a couple of crazy kids in class who are always bringing that kind of stuff into school."

Blake kept to the highroad, confident that soon they would be on their way to a relationship that was all he could possibly dream of.

Anthony was equally confident that the pressure was rising within the man. He also knew that he must have concrete evidence of what Blake had done to lead him down the path to an illicit relationship. When he had that tool he would have Blake tied to any action that he wanted him to do. He was anxious to reach that moment.

Blake seemed awkward and uncertain, but then he shrugged his head and seemed to make a decision. He looked strangely at Anthony and then pointed to several large boxes, which were clustered against a far wall of the study.

"Anthony, have you noticed the things in that corner of the room?

"Yes I have, but I didn't want to be rude and ask you about them."

"Well, they are a special pride of mine, and when you have arranged to spend the night here, I will set them up and reveal a wonderful world to you. We will skip Jane Austen and spend the evening with something that I am certain you will enjoy."

"Everything is wonderful when I am with you, Steve. I am always happy here."

"Your remarks always delight me, my dear Anthony, but it is late and I should be sending you home now.

They lingered a bit as Blake commented on how much they had accomplished with the wonderful Austen works and Anthony agreed heartily. They said their goodbyes and then Anthony started out.

But before Blake closed the door he said, "Don't forget about talking to your folks about your working one night with your fellow student."

Anthony had spun back to his teacher and embraced him in a tight bear hug as he said, "I never forget the important things, and thank you, thank you so much. You make me so happy."

He then swirled away and sped home.

The Reverend smiled at his younger self. Even then he was doing everything correctly.

Yes, it had to be the fourth meeting before Blake really made the mistake that would change his life, and put Anthony further on his path to greatness.

Chapter Ten

Their next meeting brought forth a sorrowful Anthony. When he and Blake were walking towards the study, Anthony was almost in tears as he told Blake that he wasn't sure if he could ever stay for the night.

"I had my father convinced that it would be a good thing for me to do. Then my mother asked who the kid was that I would be working with. I told her Jimmie O'Brien. Damned if she didn't almost have a delighted fit. It seemed that Mrs. O'Brien was some kind of big shot at the church. Mom desperately was trying to meet with her."

He went on with greater detail telling Steve how his mother had railed on about not having the clothes to go visiting someone like Jimmie's mother. 'No, you must have them come here. I'll straighten up the...'

At this point his father had screamed out, 'Like hell she can be coming here. I don't want anyone disturbing what I do at night or seeing this filthy house.'

Right then both Steve and Anthony knew that there was no way of pulling off his ploy.

"Now I know there is no way I can get that to happen. There just won't be any sleepovers. I am so unhappy."

"Well, you are no unhappier than I am."

Suddenly Blake jumped up with a huge smile on his face.

"I know what we are going to do tonight. We are going to forget Jane Austen and just do things that we can enjoy. First come on over to those mystery parcels I showed you last week."

They both rushed to the far side of the room where said items had remained untouched.

"You rip open the papers that are covering those long wood poles. I'll open the other box and then we will put them together."

Anthony was caught up with the excitement that engulfed Blake, but did not have an idea about what was being assembled.

It was barely a few moments before Anthony held up three stout poles, each about one meter in length. He then attached them to a flat board a bit over one quarter of a meter square.

The poles extended out about one meter apart on the floor. Atop the board was an almost square wooden box whose dimensions were about one third of a meter in height by a touch bigger in width. A circular metal shaft protruded from what seemed to be the front of this mechanism, and it had a small door that hung open from the back end.

Anthony did not have any concept about what this could be.

"Anthony, my fine feathered friend, can you guess what this is?"

"I don't have the foggiest notion."

"Do you know the name Louis Daguerre?'"

"No, I've never heard that name. Steve, please stop teasing me and tell me what this thing is."

"Daguerre is the name of a French inventor. He and several others have created a process that permits one to produce what are called photographs. What you are looking at is a camera. This camera produced photographs I want to show you. But, before I do that, let me advise you that what you see might revolt you, or it might give you great joy."

Here it was some fifty years after those sentences were uttered and the Reverend could still repeat them almost word for word.

"I want you to know that I am quite fond of you. No, it is much more than that. I am much more than fond of you. Whatever I feel for you, do know, it is more than teacher and student liking one another."

Anthony merely looked up to his friend.

"My feelings for you have rushed upon me far speedier than I would have believed. I have really known you but a few weeks, and I am about to open myself up to you in a manner that could lead to my destruction."

"Steve, you don't have to show me or tell me anything. Let me just tell you that when I first approached you, I did so because my father told me if I didn't become your friend he was going to give me the worst beating I ever had in my life. I was ready to hate you, but a crazy thing happened to me. I like you every bit as much as you say you like me."

Those words were spoken with an adult ring and a passion that overwhelmed Blake.

Blake was on the verge of crying with delight, but he had more to do in order to secure his safety. If he revealed his true thoughts and Anthony was not there with him, it could beget another reenactment of what he had endured in England. All was dependent upon how this young Irish boy would react.

"What you just said brings me infinite joy but I must tell you more. I am a man much different from anyone you have ever known. Very few people have seen what I want to show you. They reveal what I am, so I must first ask you several questions. Your answers will determine where we go from there."

"Steve, you are frightening me. I don't know what you could show me that could change my feelings about you. Other than that, I don't know what to say. I think you should let me go home right now.

"Fine, but let me tell you that what I expose to you can never be talked about with anyone other than the two of us. What is of paramount importance is that should you dislike what you will see you must immediately tell me to stop. I will never again show them to you. If you like them I will continue making them available to you. Are you brave enough for me to continue?"

"I don't know why you are putting me to this test."

With that he jumped to his feet and sped out of the house as fast as he could move.

When the door slammed on Anthony's back, tears flew down Blake's eyes.

Anthony on the other hand smiled and laughed all the way home. He knew he was but inches away from achieving his goals.

He would gladly sear this man's soul if it helped him reach his goal. There was nothing that could force him off his path. The only care he had was that Blake seemed so frightened on how to proceed. He must be certain that there was no turning back for his dear Mr. Blake.

Chapter Eleven

"Mr. Blake, in our last lesson you talked about declarative sentences. Some of us were confused. What happens, for example, if you're terribly frightened and are asked to answer some really tough question? How can you, in answering that question, deliver it as a declarative sentence?"

God, I was one brilliant young and ballsy kid. To get up in the middle of a class and pose a question that only one person could interpret correctly took much belief in oneself. To have the courage and belief that I could pull it off was, in retrospect, astounding.

But, the Reverend thought, I did pull it off and have used that same technique a hundred times since. Was it because I was so young and didn't have the experience to know what could come down on me, or was it for the fact that I was so desperate to win this battle that nothing frightened me? Probably it was a combination of both.

The image of Mr. Blake seemed to leap out as he tried to answer my question. He did a good deal of 'Ah hemming' and 'Ah yessing' and then a very long pause, before giving me the shallowest of answers.

"I believe that question would have been quite fitting for yesterday's class but doesn't fit in with what we are now working on. If you, and any of you other students who are also interested, could stop by at the end of class today, I'll be more than happy to answer all your questions."

Word spread quickly around the school of how Anthony had made Blake look like a blithering idiot who had to have the time to look up how to answer a question.

Anthony's back was slapped by practically every boy in the school, and loud cheers echoed through the building praising the victory of the students over that stuffy old teacher.

Of course, at the end of the day, every soul other than Anthony deserted the building. He, instead, walked very sheepishly into Blake's classroom.

Very severely, Blake pronounced, "Well, my dear Mr. O'Donnell, shall we wait until all the others join us, or is this to be just you and me?"

"No sir, as we both knew, they've all raced home."

"Am I correct in saying that your question had not one thing to do with school work but was just a cover for personal questions between the two us?"

"Yes, sir, as usual you are right. I wanted you to know that I was ready to answer the question you posed the other night. I am now ready to give you that answer."

"If I am correct in what I think you are saying, don't you believe this is not the time or place for us to discuss the matter? Why don't we meet later this afternoon at my house where we can safely go into all facets of what you have to say?"

Anthony ended further conversation with a soft reply.

"I'll be there in one hour."

Chapter Twelve

This was no time to pity that absurd teacher. Indeed, as the young boy had rationalized it, he was bringing a bit of happiness into that ugly man's life. Blake desperately needed male companionship, but Cork, and his job at the school prevented even the slightest venturing into the life he desired.

That poor, silly little man. Anthony wondered for a brief second if he had gone too far. Then again, he was a young lad desperately searching for a path to, as yet, undiscovered happiness. What had to be done, had to be done.

"I realize that you need me even more than I need you, so I am here to see whatever you want me to see and to do whatever you want me to do."

If ever there was a happy man, it was this glowing man looking up at Anthony. This man with the terrible teeth, far from handsome face and shortness of stature, thanking God for blessing him with this giant of a boy, who soon would be delighting him in a manner he desperately yearned for.

"Anthony, I prayed that you would come back to me with those words."

He then took Anthony by the hand and led him back to the study.

"Now I want you to go into the study by yourself. On my desk you will find many pictures. I am very proud of those pictures. They all were taken by the equipment I showed you last time. All but one will be turned face down. And, let me ask you one more time. Are you absolutely positive that you want to go on with this?"

"I couldn't be more certain of anything."

"All right then. What I am about to show you will be something I am certain you have never seen. I want you to look at the one that is face up. It may shock you or stun you. If you like it and want to see more, shout out and I will immediately join you. If, on the other hand, you dislike what it shows, just leave here and go home. And we will end our meetings forever."

It all seemed mysterious but Anthony nodded, opened the door and walked in. There indeed was one picture facing up. Anthony picked it up and quietly laughed. He stared at it for some time all the while knowing that what he held in his hand was his passport to Dublin and college.

The picture showed a naked Blake and another naked man performing an act that was either the most grievous sin or a glorification of a pleasure that certain men enjoyed.

He waited several moments and then shouted out, "Steve, please come in."

Anthony seemed a little shaken when he waved the picture at Blake.

"Did you love this man?"

"No, this was a need being satisfied for the both of us. Love never entered our doing what we did. Did we love what we were doing? Yes, absolutely. Do I want to do the same with you? Yes, of course, but this time my love for you will be of paramount importance."

"As you said, I was more than a little shocked when I first looked at it. It is all so strange to me. I know that I feel differently about you than any other person. And that is good, but I am confused as well. Please, let me have a little time to think more about this. I promise, I will be back tomorrow afternoon, and we can go on from there. Oh, may I take this picture home and study it? I guarantee you that no one else will ever see it"

"Without a doubt you can. But bring it back with you. My life is in your hands, but I trust you will not show it to anyone else.

"They would have to kill me before I showed it to anyone."

With that he hugged Blake and gave him their first kiss. They both clung to each other and then Anthony broke it off and left.

Chapter Thirteen

The following day, just before lunch break would end, Blake was putting some school papers together. He had had a most pleasant day and was in a very good mood as he quietly whistled away while performing this terribly dull task.

He had been extra kind to all of his students and they, in turn, were all wondering what had happened to their usual sharp-tongued monster of a teacher.

He was just about to leave his office when Anthony walked in.

"Steve, can I steal a little of your time?"

"Well, isn't this a nice surprise. But this isn't a good place to talk. Why don't we go to my house after school as usual?"

"Because I don't think we will ever be going back to your house again."

"I'm confused. What are you saying?"

"I tell you what. Why don't we take a little walk, and I will explain it all to you."

A much puzzled and disturbed English teacher stared at his favorite student but couldn't come up with anything to counter these rather roughly offered words.

"It won't take long. I'll start walking towards the shops down the street and pretend to be looking through the windows. You can join me there, and we will walk off as if we didn't know one another."

And with that he abruptly turned from his teacher and headed out. Five minutes later he was at the chemist's shoppe. Within two minutes, he spied Mr. Blake headed his way.

Anthony started out again and made a left turn down the next street. Mr. Blake was soon at his side.

Anthony immediately began to slow his pace and, in a most assured tone, said the following.

"I've decided that I want to go to Trinity College in Dublin, and I've come up with a sure fire plan on how to get there. And, you are going to be my prime asset in getting me the credentials to get there."

Somewhat relieved but still puzzled Blake said, "Of course, I would love to help you in any way I can, but why are you so bristly today?"

"Me, bristly? Oh no. I couldn't be happier. Let me tell you what you are going to do starting immediately"

Blake was somewhat frightened by this command which came out so forcefully.

"It is very simple. I will advise you whenever I have a test coming up in any subject. You will then get a copy of that test and give it to me with all the correct answers. My grades are pretty good now, but, together, we are going to see to it that all my grades come out as the best they could possibly be."

Mr. Blake reared up and screamed out. "What the hell did you just say?"

"Just shut up and listen carefully. In addition to what you will do with all my tests, you will also write a letter of commendation that proclaims my love of study and the unquestioned brilliance of mind. I don't care what words you use. Just make certain that the message gets out. Oh yes, you will also get as many of your fellow teachers to write the same sort of letter about what a stellar student I am."

By this time Blake was near hysteria. Who was this creature who was screaming at him? Where was the Anthony who yesterday loved him? Why in the name of hell must he tolerate this dreadful verbal abuse?

"Now the second part of your job in this project is difficult, but I am certain you will be able to secure it for me. Though Trinity will not cost me any money, I will need money to live on. I am told that those funds are available for needy students. God knows, I will be the neediest one in all of Dublin. Do you have any questions?"

Blake could hardly breathe, but he managed to get out one sentence, "I will never be a part of anything like that."

"Don't be silly. Of course you will. Do you recall showing me some very strange pictures the other day? I am sure you do. Well, I still have the one you gave me and, you should know that your house was broken into today and, strangely enough the only thing taken was a lot of equally naughty pictures. But, in fairness, I should tell you that I placed four of the best pictures in different parts of your house. If all goes well, I will tell you where they are hidden."

Blake nearly fell over. His heart was beating faster than it ever had. Perspiration kept falling from his face, but he seemed to be shivering from a cold wave that had swept over his body.

"Don't think I will not be grateful for all you are going to do for me. I would never reveal your secret, and you will be through with me in two or three years. The only thing that might anger me enough to harm you would be if you failed in any part of your job. If I do receive the financial support I need to attend Trinity, I will return each of what is so precious to you.

Blake could not get out another word. He managed to stay erect by holding himself up against a wall they stood at.

"Obviously, if I don't receive your best efforts and I don't get into Trinity, who knows if those pictures might reappear in the hands of people you certainly do not want to see them. Should they fall into those hands, think of how disdainfully they will be viewed. Do you clearly understand me?"

A destroyed Blake nodded. His body seemed to fold into an even smaller body than he normally presented to the public.

"Now let me tell you two other things. Don't try to run away from this. If you do so, I will tell my father what he dragged me into and give him those pictures. He will either kill you or have the constabulary doing what they do so well to your type. If, on the other hand, you do all I ask, you will have a friend for life, willing to help you in any way I can."

Ever so slowly Blake began to cry and with the tears covering his face, he lost all strength and started sliding down from the wall.

Ever so gently Anthony picked him up and dusted off his clothes.

"Well this has been very pleasant. Just know that I want you to stay here in Cork and prosper. I really do like you, and you really have taught me much. In fact I want to start working with you on the way I speak. By the time I go to Trinity I want to be speaking as if I were a fine English gentleman."

Blake managed to stand straight and Anthony gave him the assistance he needed to walk to the corner.

"Oh yes, one last thing. Don't even think of suicide or some other stupid stunt like that. We wouldn't want to embarrass your family with the dire news of what their beloved son was."

Chapter Fourteen

Thoughts of suicide or the possibility of telling all to the headmaster flashed through his mind daily. However, the vision of facing the senior O'Donnell who would, without a doubt, torture him before killing him, left but one choice. He must go along with Anthony's hideous proposal.

The one grace afforded the poor man was that there were no important tests on the immediate horizon for Anthony.

He decided to spring a surprise quiz on Anthony's English class. The evening before said test he slipped a sheet of paper to Anthony on which all the answers were listed.

Much groaning came forth from the class with the exception of Anthony, who shouted out what an easy test it was.

In the teacher's lounge that afternoon, Blake raved to one and all that, once again, Anthony had scored one hundred percent on an unannounced quiz. The closest mark to him was about seventy-two percent.

"I tell you that kid is a bloody genius. I think I should prepare one test for him and an easier one for the others. Is he as bright in your classes as well?"

Each of the teachers noted that he was bright when he wanted to be, but far too often didn't seem to give a damn about their class.

"You know, he was just that way in my class, but I think he is changing. He even has started asking pertinent questions of me. Let's watch and see if he is as bright as I think he is."

After class the next day, he asked Anthony to stay for a few minutes. Several of the other students lingered by to hear Mr. Blake praise Anthony and his new approach to learning.

"I've even spoken to my fellow teachers and they said you were certainly bright, but they would like to see more involvement from you in the daily class work. You've got a brain there, Mr. O'Donnell, let others see it as well as I do."

With that he turned his back to Anthony, blithely ignoring the catcalls that fell on Anthony from all of his hysterical classmates.

Anthony's response to his fellow classmates was to drag the strongest one out behind the school and give him a beating the boy would never forget.

"Now if any of you other hooligans even think of laughing at me, I want you to remember how sad this piece of shite looks."

Never again would Anthony hear anything but hosannas from anyone in the school.

Later Blake pronounced sternly to Anthony, "It is time for you, Mr. Anthony, to get off your ass and go to work. This is a full time battle, and you have to be ready to fight on all fronts. The most important part of getting each of the teachers to like and admire you is that you show them how hard you are working."

With those words his old pal Steve had told him two things. The first was that Blake had started doing what

Anthony asked him to do. But the second was even more important. In order to succeed, it was not Blake or anyone else, but Anthony himself who must gear up for a long and tough war.

Anthony gave himself a one sentence speech.

"It's all in my hands now. Let's see if I am man enough to make it happen."

His new approach to learning was soon noted by all of his teachers. He became a joy to those teachers who really cared about teaching. Most every adult in the school was delighted with the progress of this young genius, and some went so far as to give Anthony, of their own free will, hints on what the questions would be on the upcoming tests.

The headmaster himself had told each of his staff of the value they had in this young Irish lad.

"He can be of great worth to the reputation of our school. We will be the ultimate beneficiaries, as word gets out about our teaching prowess."

To those who couldn't have given a damn whether he learned or didn't, he was an unforgiving horror. He would pepper them with question after question, and if he did not like their answers, he had a stock response.

"There's a hole in your ass ya silly horse cart so stop handing out that poop and give me a real answer."

Chapter Fifteen

In contrast to how well things were progressing for Anthony, Ireland was sinking deeper and deeper into the agonies of the famine. The word that the famine was all but over floated throughout the country, but the rate of deaths, and the number of people fleeing Ireland, continued unabated.

This ever-rising loss of people throughout Cork left in its wake a broken city. The school system was, at its best, bedraggled.

The ever benevolent English initiated a program of Workhouses. It, in English eyes, was the humane way of helping those, poor, lost Irishmen.

In reality, it destroyed almost every family that entered its confines. Education was a foreign word that was not to be discussed. Its school program lacked teachers and books. In reality, it was merely a storage facility for young children who had been separated from their families.

Anthony was, of course, aware of all of this. It drove him to an important decision. Since the English were the winners, and the Irish, all but dead losers, he would, as soon as he could, be deleting the O' from his name. Then he would not be just another damned Irishman and become the handsome Englishman, Anthony Angus Donnell.

Chapter Sixteen

The next year just flew by with nary a snag for Anthony, as Mr. Blake became an open warrior for his towering young friend.

Blake was confident that he and the boy were friends again. Not in the total manner that Blake desired, but as mutual conspirators striking out to achieve what Anthony had initiated.

Though their meetings were no longer held at his home, they would, at least twice a week, meet and walk the back streets of Cork. The primary purpose of these strolls was to work on Anthony's speech patterns. This was moving ahead splendidly.

At home Anthony became almost a mute. No one there would gather why Anthony was sounding so strangely, as Anthony less and less slipped into his native brogue.

Blake had taken charge of all activities at the school, and soon the entire faculty was raving about the young genius they had given birth to. Correspondence with Trinity was ongoing.

The headmaster himself joined the fray and became Anthony's leading advocate. There had never been a single student to graduate from this little school in Cork and then move on to the most prestigious college in all of Ireland.

He went out of his way to spread the word of the young genius he and his fellow teachers had nurtured at their school. At many a social event or educational meeting, he could be heard talking of this wonder child they had developed.

"I tell you that in all my years of teaching, I have never met such a natural scholar. I am so proud of how my teachers have turned that fertile brain into a mind that just grows and grows."

As he neared his eighteenth birthday, his mum had somehow managed to bake a tiny cake honoring that event. Unfortunately, the birthday was on a Friday and Anthony's father arrived home dead sober and at his meanest.

For whatever reason, as soon as he entered the house, he took a wild swing at Grace. He missed his mark and spun around. Clearly off balance he landed near Anthony who grabbed his father's arm and twisted it into a tortuous grip.

"Hey, dear Father, let's you and I go out for a bit of a walk."

To see his father take a swing at Grace brought Anthony to an anger level well beyond simple fury.

Another fearsome twist elicited a scream from the older O'Donnell, as Anthony dragged him out of the house. Once outside, Anthony threw his father to the ground and gave his father a full strength kick in the face which all but knocked the man out.

With one hand, Anthony tore off his father's belt and then hit him with another foot smashing into his face. He then tied the man's hands with his belt and then he knelt with his knees jammed into his father's neck.

"Dear Father, I've got news for you. That swing at Grace was the last swing at any of us that you are ever going to take. Now I know you are sober, so I know you can hear me. So listen up."

Anthony rose up and then hit out with another kick that was aimed and delivered at the kidney of the man lying prone beneath him. The resultant scream seemed to echo throughout the countryside.

"If you ever try to get back at me, I will beat you silly and throw you to drown in the sea. And if you try to beat Mom, or any of the others in our family, you will get the same treatment. You are an old and stupid man, but you will also be a dead man if you ever, and I mean ever, do anything like raising your hand against anyone in this family."

Anthony then rose and left his father lying in a dirt patch.

The beating he had just given out was horrendous, but what was even more terrifying was that this little speech was delivered, purposely, in almost perfect English.

The man lay on the ground in fearful pain, but his mind kept shouting out, *'Who the hell was that who beat me so badly?'*

Anthony went back to a brief but rousing reception from all in the family. But the cheers were quickly silenced by his mother.

"Just shut up you packa fools."

With one hand she pointed to the oldest boys in the room and ordered them to bring their father in. She then, with all her might, slapped Anthony in the face.

"Are you crazy? You filthy gurrrier. Don't you know you've just taken everything away from that poor man? It would have been better if you had killed him. If he can't rule things in this pathetic house, what is he? You aren't worth living you stupid twat."

And with that, she once again hit Anthony across his face. And, to add to her obvious hatred of the boy, she spat in his face.

"Now, get out of my sight. I never want to see that ugly face of yours ever again."

Yes, the blows stung Anthony, but he did not utter a word. He looked at his mother and was stunned at the anger and contempt that was pouring from her.

He stood looking at her as she turned from him, dampened a cloth, and then ran out towards her husband. Why wasn't she thanking him for saving Grace? Wasn't it time that somebody told his fool of a father that striking others was over and done with?

Anthony watched the boys place their father in his bed and heard his mother softly telling her lord and master that he would be just fine as she ever so gently washed his face. As she bent over to kiss the man, Anthony turned and went to the corner of the room where he gathered up the few things he owned and the Jane Austen books.

Chapter Seventeen

Anthony tore out the front door, keeping his eyes focused ahead. His face still felt the sting of his mother's hand, and he was ablaze with anger. He had no idea as to where he was going, but he was certain of one fact. He was bang on certain that his future would never again include this house, or anyone inside it.

Anthony kept a very rapid pace as he pushed his way from the only home he had ever known. He kept rethinking of what had just occurred, and he was as confused as any seventeen-year old could be.

He had simply gone to the defense of his sister. Yes, he had beaten his father but that was long overdue, for a man who had spent the last thirty years beating up on people without even a thought of payment for the pain he had inflicted on all of his family.

And what does his mother do? She defends a man who had never done anything but agonize everyone close to him. Who does she blame? By her actions it was obviously her youngest child!

Not that old bastard, but the boy she had lovingly named after her father -- the one with the courage to show his love for that poor lost sister of his. And all her fury was vented against that same boy.

Is the world crazy? No logical answer came to him.

There was no place to hide. Nothing but an ever darkening sky, a swirling sea and what looked like a rain storm ready to descend on him.

He must have walked for about a half-hour before he stopped. He found himself at the edge of the sea. He did not know how he had gotten there nor why he had come this way.

There was no one near that he could talk to.

He could hide in the church, but if they found him there, he knew they would send him back to his house, which was the last place in the world that he wanted to ever return to.

There was no friend, no relative, no one to turn to. The one person he loved obviously detested him and that thought brought forth copious tears. His normal sense of courage, or was it braggadocio, disappeared. He did not have anywhere he could turn to.

He lay on the ground hoping that lightning would strike down and kill him. And, at the height of his misery, he recalled one man who had once liked him. Possibly he could still rely on the man named Stephen Blake.

"Yes, he'll forgive me. He'll understand. Blake will save me."

He picked himself off the ground and tried to gather heart. Yet the rapid pace which had pushed him away from his house began to slow. At times, it seemed like he was barely moving. He kept repeating the phrase, 'Blake will save me.' But his pace kept growing slower and slower.

The thought grew that his plea for help would be laughed at and derided by Blake. Doubt began to creep into his mind.

Why should he help me after what I have done to him? But step by step, he grew closer and closer to Blake's home.

He hadn't proceeded more than half a mile when the promised rain started pouring down on him. He barely felt the water that was engulfing him and swirled over every part of his body.

But, he kept moving forward. And the next thing he knew he was on his hands and knees looking up at Blake's front door.

His mind was in turmoil. Outwardly, he looked dreadful, while inwardly, he was in an even more ghastly state. But somehow, his fist hit the door, at first timidly, and then harder and with more despair.

It seemed as if the door would never open, but, in fact, it was merely a moment or two before the door opened, and there stood Blake. The man who must become his savior!

"My God, what are doing here? No, just get in here."

Anthony fell through the doorway and lay on the floor looking up to Blake.

"I know you hate me, and there is every reason why you should. But, I couldn't think of anyone else who might help me. Please let me stay just tonight."

Blake did not respond but instead dashed off to immediately return with a handful of towels. He dried Anthony as well as he could and then tore off all the boys drenched garments and clothed him in a heavy woolen bathrobe.

Not a word passed between the two until that task was done. "Now get into my study while I get some tea on."

Anthony did not respond, but instead dug into his belongings. From that wet mass, he pulled out a large envelope. It was the same parcel of pictures that he had previously stolen from Blake.

Blake immediately recognized the packet but took no notice of them. He offered no comment other than, "As I said, get into the studio and I'll be right there with some food."

It took just a bit and he entered the studio carrying a tray full of hot tea, a bit of a ham sandwich and a dozen large cookies.

Anthony lay on the carpet and in his hand he held out the packet which Blake had ignored. But, still, not a word from him.

Blake took the packet threw it onto his desk and said, "First you eat, and then we talk."

Anthony was certain that he could not eat a thing, but he did try a bit of the sandwich, and then a sip of the tea, and before long there wasn't a morsel left on the plate.

And then, for the second time, Anthony's face was flooded with tears that flowed down his face. This was not some sham play by the boy but the sign of total defeat. He was no longer the arrogant person who would rule the world.

"Now, calm down. Wipe your face, and, when you are ready, tell me what has happened."

It was a good five minutes before the first coherent words came forth.

"I... I... I thought I could handle everything but I'm wrong. I'm just a loud mouth with a dream that I will never be able to pull off."

Again the tears burst forth.

"No. You are talking nonsense. Now start again and slowly tell me everything."

Blake's soft spoken enthusiasm brought a bit of confidence to Anthony and, ever so slowly, the entire story emerged. His full blown hatred for his father dotted almost every sentence. But, getting to his mother's actions was a far more difficult task.

"Steve, did you love your mother and did she love you?"

"Yes, I loved her very much, and she loved me too. I was about your age when I told her of my problems. She said nothing would ever change her opinion of me, but that I should never tell my father or my brothers. She became my confidant and enabled me to get on fairly well."

"You were very lucky."

"Even when I fell into trouble and had to leave England, she gave me the courage to go on. I still receive a loving letter from her each week. In each letter she sends me many English pounds. I couldn't exist on the measly salary the school pays. With what she doles out to me, I live very well and can even save money each week. Why do you ask?"

With much difficulty, Anthony managed to tell of his mother's actions after he had beaten his father.

"I beat my father as much for her as I did for all the rest of us. But here was the one person I thought really cared for me and her response was to show how much she hated me. If she hates me, there isn't a person who cares for me. I could be dead and no one would give a damn about it."

"You are wrong Anthony. I still care for you."

"I don't understand. I could not have done anything more terrible to you even though you were always so nice to me."

"Oh, don't think I didn't want to kill you for being such a conniving bastard, but, as things progressed, I got to like the game I was playing. There isn't a soul at that school that I admire, particularly the Head Master and as I saw him fall so easily into the trap you had opened, my delight with the whole adventure just grew and grew. I was having more fun than I have ever had."

He took a minute to stare at Anthony. He recalled how he at first would have gladly killed the boy. But that was not what Blake was like. And when he started to see what this was really all about, he had let the enjoyment be the motivator of his actions.

"And, though I believed you had led me on terribly, I admired the way you pulled it off. And, I might have been a fool, but I felt that you would never release those pictures, because you, in your own style, did like me a small bit."

"No, Steve, let me now be honest. I did like you a little bit because you could not have been nicer to me, but I wouldn't give them the pictures for another selfish reason. I still thought I could use them in some other scheme that I might dream up. Like everything else, it was all about what would have been best for me."

"And now what is it that you want me to do?"

"Just please let me spend the night here. I don't have a thought beyond that. I promise I'll leave tomorrow, and you will never see me again."

Blake poured himself a cup of tea. He sipped away while looking at the boy who stared back at his teacher and wondered what the man was thinking.

"No, Anthony, that isn't good for either of us. I am now as much vested in your plan as you are. In fact, I do believe I want to pull this off more than you do. Somehow, somehow..."

And, in mid sentence he stopped talking and started nodding his head.

"Yes, I think that could work. Anthony, listen up and tell me what you think of the following."

He paused again to mentally play out one more time the thought he had just come up with.

"Yes, this can work Anthony. My housekeeper, Mrs. Rafferty, is almost starving to death. She is really a pleasant old lady who doesn't have a friend or a relative who hasn't died in the horror we all live in. She is the typical starving-to-death Irish woman. I think working for me is the only job she has, and she is going to lose the tiny house she now lives in. What say I ask her to come live with me?"

"What has that got to do with my staying tonight?"

"Oh, of course you can stay tonight. I'm talking about you staying every night. You can share the spare bedroom with her. And she will take care of both of us."

"As much as I owe you, I don't want to be what you are."

"For goodness sake, wake up. Forget about what you think I want of you. That is history, and there is no chance in hell that those thoughts might ever arise again. But, you and Mrs. Rafferty need me and, I guess, I need the two of you. Let's give it a try. I think it could work out just fine."

There was still no visible reaction, in one way or the other, from Anthony.

"Listen closely. I am sure of what I am saying. Mrs. Rafferty will be the happiest old woman in the world. You will be able to still attend school, while your family won't have a clue as to where you are. And I will be living once again with a family that needs me. Come on, Anthony, we are going to have a grand time until we ship you off to Dublin."

"But what if she doesn't want to live here? And what are you going to tell her about me?"

"Believe me, she will be delirious with happiness when she moves in. She has been hinting for weeks now about my letting her live here, and if you just speak kindly to her, and show you care for her, she will adore you. The more we ask her to do for us, the happier she will be. She is a born mother and will soon be running our lives in a manner that she thinks is suitable."

Anthony's frown of negativity slowly disappeared. It was replaced by a wide grin. Finally he stood up.

"Steve, we are going to be having more fun than is legal in this stupid country."

Chapter Eighteen

Anthony kept hearing an enormously loud screeching in his head. It certainly sounded like a woman's voice, but it couldn't be coming from Grace who hardly ever spoke or his mother who, even when she was at her angriest, never spoke in a loud voice.

Slowly he began to decipher the words which seemed to be saying something like 'Get the red out or you'll be late to drool and Mr. Blake will be heavy sad.'

One eye opened and the other followed suit. They revealed a tiny and very fragile looking woman screaming out at him.

"Did you say something about being late for school and red made Mr. Blake very angry? And, oh, are you Mrs. Rafferty?"

"Well who the divil else should I be? He told me all about you. So, Lord Anthony, get your holy Joe fat backside out of bed this very second or Master Blake will be very mad at me."

"What are you doing here so early in the morning?"

"Mother above, protect me from the ignorance of this child. Here Mr. Blake has only just finished telling me how smart you are, and I find a dullard sharing my bedroom. Do listen to what I'll be saying to ya. I got thrown out of my house late yesterday, so last night I came here just like you did. You were fast asleep when I got here. We were both looking for the man to save us. And he did."

Within minutes he washed his face, got dressed and stood warily facing this tiny terror standing next to him.

"Being the dear man he always is, he just said that you were in a pack of trouble and needed help. But you can't fool me. I am sure you are just another punk Irish troublemaker. So let me tell you, if you give him one bit of grief, I'll either chop your head off or do the same to your bollocks. Do you understand?

"Oh yes, Maam, I do, and if I do anything to hurt Mr. Blake, I'll welcome your doing whatever you want to do to me. Where is he now?"

"He had some special work to do so he left real early. He told me to give you a little more time in bed and then make you get up and right off to school. So I've got a nice cup of tea for you and cookies you can eat on your way there.

Anthony tasted the tea, took a bite of the cookies and then pronounced. 'I'm going to love that old bat. She's the most honest person I have ever met.'

Chapter Nineteen

Blake's sexual desires for Anthony were long since gone and forgotten by both him and the young man. That was replaced with a true love affair between the two. It was as if Steve had become a proud father, and Anthony had found a father he could respect and admire.

Anthony had even confided to Steve his promise to treat everyone like an enemy and to use said enemy as a stepping stone to success--the exact way he had treated his relationship with Blake.

Though he totally disagreed with that philosophy, Blake wrote it off as mere youthful anger, but he understood the forces that had driven Anthony down that path. The more he thought of it, the more he believed it was the correct path for Anthony to travel down at this stage of his life.

Blake was committed to becoming a lifelong advisor to Anthony who, on his part, knew that whatever Steve said was meant to further his chances for the huge success story he must pursue.

It was late into Anthony's senior year in school when Blake approached him. He was holding an envelope addressed to Anthony.

"Anthony, we have had a great relationship and I have enjoyed every bit of it, but we have for almost two years avoided one thing that must be done. And it must be done as quickly as possible."

"I am not sure I like the tone you are taking. What have I not done that is so serious?"

"Sit down, shut up, and listen to me."

With that, Blake revealed that he was positive that soon Anthony would be off for Dublin and Trinity College. He also felt that Anthony would never return to Cork. He furthermore knew that there was something that he and Anthony had neglected to do. It was an act that must be performed.

"Yesterday, I went by your old house. Your mother was on her hands and knees in that tiny potato patch trying, I believe, to find a potato or two that was edible. I introduced myself. I told her that I was a teacher and was wandering by, and when I came upon this house, I recalled coming upon this very spot not too long ago to see a young student of mine."

He then told of the woman looking up at him with very mean eyes and shouting out that none of her children were in school.

"She then went on to tell me that she was not in the mood for talking and to get on with my walk and don't be bothering her. She added on the warning that her husband would soon be home from work and that if I didn't stop acting like a 'culchie' and get the hell out of there, she would have her husband beat me silly.'"

"Well, Steve, doesn't that prove everything I've told you of them is true. They are monsters, and I don't know why you even went up there."

"Because you must do something that may give pleasure to that pitiful woman and because it may save you from self-hatred. I don't want you to ever wake up with any sense of remorse about never saying goodbye to your mother."

Anthony raised a fist as he shouted, "You are mad. I hate them all…" but Steve quickly drowned him out.

"Shut up, and listen to me. This letter is from Trinity College. I've read it. It is the answer to your dreams. It says that you have been accepted to enroll there this coming September."

Anthony just stood there with his mouth agape and his arms hanging limply at his sides.

"I fully understand the hatred you bear for your family. But I don't want you to even think of leaving here without going to your mother and ask her forgiveness for what has happened."

"I will never do that."

"Well then I will have to do something that I detest even thinking about. I want you to rethink your answer right here and now. If you do not change your feelings, I will be forced to do something that will hurt you and hurt me equally."

"What can you do that will hurt us so badly?"

"Either you change your mind about going to see your mother, and with good thoughts in the doing of same, or I will rip up this letter and advise my friends there that it is impossible for you to ever come to Dublin."

"You couldn't do that."

"Once again, hear me out. You will do what I say, and do so because you know it is the correct thing to do. If you choose otherwise, the letter will be shredded the minute you answer me incorrectly. You've got this evening to make your decision."

Anthony turned pale and a strange puzzlement came over him.

"You heard me. Don't think you will be able to blackmail me or use some phony verbal agreement to prevent me from destroying this letter. I am going out at seven this evening to have dinner at the headmaster's home. When I return, I will expect to hear your decision."

With that he stalked away. He was furious.

Exactly one hour later Anthony knocked at Steve's door.

"Come in."

"I've thought it out, and, as usual, I thought in terms of what is best for me. I am tired of saying my mother and my father is this or that. So I have decided to go to them with you. I'll try and apologize for being such a self-centered bastard and never thinking of how tough life has been for them. I doubt that any good will come of this, but I am more than willing to try."

Blake did not say a word. He just kept staring at Anthony.

"Please believe me I am not saying this so that I can go to Trinity or to please you."

He more than choked up at this point and had to take an extended pause.

"I am doing this to please myself and never have to have negative thoughts about myself. Hopefully, I can get a little bonus by bringing a little happiness into their lives and seeing them smile for the first time in my life. But, I don't want anyone to ever pity me for being what I am. And there is not one lie in anything I have just said."

And Blake knew that the words were true as he had bet himself they would be.

Chapter Twenty

The next day, possibly a few minutes after five, Blake and Anthony slowly approached the dilapidated house that the O'Donnells called home. Anthony was the most frightened he had ever been as he looked upon this house that he hated so much.

They carried with them several parcels of food, a new hat for Anthony's mother, a spring coat for his father and various dresses and shoes for Grace.

There was no one in sight in either the field or in front of the front door.

Blake walked to the door with Anthony just behind him. Knocking on the door produced no response. He called out, "Mr. O'Donnell, Mrs. O'Donnell, could you please come to the door."

Still, not a word came from behind the door.

"Steve, let me try something. Hey, Grace, open the door. I'm loaded down with packages for you. Come on, Grace, you'll love what I have for you."

The door still did not open, but they did hear a sort of shuffling from within the building.

A hushed conversation confirmed that there were people inside. Whether or not the front door would open, remained an unfulfilled question.

"Grace, you are going to love the cookies we have."

These magic words reached someone, for the door slowly was unlatched and Grace peeked out. She stared at Blake and looked at Anthony.

Her delighted voice screamed out, "Anthony, oh Anthony, is that really you. You're not dead. Oh, Anthony, I missed you so much.

With that the door was flung wide open and Grace roared past Blake, jumped into Anthony's open arms and smothered him with kisses, while knocking all the packages he carried to the ground.

"Where have you been? I've dreamt about you almost every night. You're going away made a bag of every day. You botched up my whole life. But now you're back, and I will never let you leave again."

What brought tears to Anthony's eyes was not the words she spoke but the thinness of her arms. Her body seemed like that of a twelve year old, not of a woman of almost twenty. He truly could not recognize the sister he once vowed to protect for her entire life. She seemed as if she was on the edge of death.

Anthony clung to his sister and matched her kiss for kiss.

"And I've missed you too. But now we're together again, and we can smile and laugh. Do you remember how I used to tickle you? You would scream and run away from me and then run back for more tickling."

"But nobody tickles me anymore, and I haven't laughed since you left."

At this point a scrawny old woman came out. Anthony looked at this woman who only slightly resembled his mother.

A tired voice said, "You're looking fine, Anthony. I am sorry we aren't doing as well as you are. Now, we'll take all your packages, and then you and your friend can get the hell out of here. Come back as often as you like with as much food as you can carry, but just leave it at the doorway. Neither me nor Grace need to see you ever again."

A horrendous scream of 'no' from Grace chilled every part of Anthony's body. She held on to him with all the strength she could muster.

"Anthony, don't listen to her. You must stay and tickle me. I need you, and I am not going to let you go."

Blake took the packages that Anthony had dropped and brought them, and the packages he carried, into the kitchen space. The others watched as he carefully laid them on the kitchen table.

He then turned to the three who were still outside and spoke directly and strongly to Anthony's mother.

"Yes, as you obviously need it, we will continue to bring you all the food you could possibly need. But, in exchange, we are taking Grace with us. So, Anthony, gather her up, and let's get going."

A wondrous smile covered Anthony's face, as he kept bobbing his head up and down in agreement with Blake's unbelievable words.

"Good. And you, Mrs. O'Donnell, what are your thoughts on the matter? I am certain that it will be better for all of us if we follow through with what I just said."

The woman slowly looked from Grace to Anthony as they clung to each other. She then looked to Blake and then back again to Grace and Anthony.

She stood there for what seemed a lifetime but did not utter a single word. She stared intently at the three in front of her and then, with her back as rigid as it could be, she simply turned from them and, as she entered her house, firmly slammed shut the front door.

Those outside could hear her turn the latch that locked them from her. Anthony, with a face full of tears, turned to Blake and the words 'Thank you, thank you,' fell from his mouth. He then picked up his sister and walked away.

There were no three people in all of Ireland who were as happy as Grace, Anthony and Steve.

Chapter Twenty One

Anthony Angus O'Donnell readied to board the train in Cork with a large smile on his face. He carried a very small bag of clothes. He had never felt grander, bigger or stronger or more confident of himself.

He gave Grace a hug she would never forget. Kissed Mrs. Rafferty and told her to take good care of Grace and Mr. Blake.

"I would not be taking this trip if it weren't for you, Steve. I will be your lifelong friend."

Blake had done all the work necessary in securing the necessary funding Anthony would need. This included enough for a limited food budget, and his rental of the tiny room he would share in a house for beginning students.

Blake would also provide monthly cash supplements that allowed for a special meal or two every other week. It was hardly luxurious living, but it did allow Anthony freedom from any financial worries.

Grace kept kissing him while tears coursed down her face. Mrs. Rafferty, ever the practical woman, loaded him down with three boxes of the finest cookies that had ever been baked.

Steve Blake handed him two envelopes while getting Anthony to promise that its contents, much currency, would only be used in an emergency.

But the reality of going off by himself had hit hard a week before his departure date. Oddly enough it was his biggest supporter, Steve Blake, who initiated the first of the problems that Anthony would encounter.

"Anthony, I do envy you your next few months in that glorious city. Dublin is full of energy and excitement and all sorts of wonders."

"But you'll be there with me for the first few weeks so you'll be a part of it all."

"No, Anthony, I've changed my mind. It's time for you to face the world yourself."

"Wait right there. That isn't what we agreed upon. I need you there for just a little while. Ya must come with me."

"No Anthony. The better and faster way is for you to go it alone. And, by the way, how many times have I told you to stop saying 'YA' when you mean to say 'YOU?' Remember you are not some stupid Irish ruffian."

"That has nothing to do with your not coming to Dublin with me."

"Wrong, wrong, wrong. It has everything to do with that. Even more to the point, you will be tested over and over again, and from the very first you will have to be able to handle it all. You are tough enough to overcome any obstacles. It is not going to be easy. But, I'm betting on you. Remember you're a winner. Don't disappoint me."

Blake steadfastly withstood all of Anthony's pleas which ranged from, 'Just spend the first week with me' to 'Then I don't care if I ever see you again.'

Blake knew that was just the old Anthony trying to get his way by conning the 'enemy.' His final words sealed the deal.

"If you can't win this little battle, how in the name of all that's holy will you fulfill your promise to be the most successful man in the world?"

The ever-present Mrs. Rafferty ended all further talk with a grand suggestion.

"I have the perfect answer for both of ya. Instead of Mr. Blake going with Anthony, Gracie and I will be with ya and, if we like it there, we might just spend a couple of months with ya in Dublin."

Blake fell to the floor weeping with laughter but managed to get out, "What a lovely thought, don't you..." but the laughter burbling from him drowned out the remainder of the sentence which was something like, "Don't you agree, Anth..." before he rolled over on his back trying to breathe rather than speak.

Anthony tried to present a solid response for Mrs. Rafferty, but the vision of him and the two ladies roaming Dublin together flashed out, and he too was on the floor with the laughter wiping away each breath he tried to take.

After some time, the two men managed to compose themselves. They both rose and dusted off their clothes. Each of them turned to face the women. Blake tried to commend dear Mrs. Rafferty but only managed to say, 'I think that is a brilliant...' before falling back to the floor and allowing the laughter to properly suffocate him.

Anthony did not do much better but managed to put forth that it might be easier if he first surveyed Dublin to see if it was a fit place for these two proper women.

He helped Blake stand up and, nodding to him, gave in to the better thinking of the man. He would do it alone.

When the time came to actually board the train, he was, surprisingly, full of confidence. He took one step up into the train and then turned back to the group beneath him.

"I am scared to death, but I promise you, I will make you all proud of me. I love you all to death, and I kiss you for making this happen."

Chapter Twenty Two

The entire Irish railway system had only been open since 1834 and its Cork line some ten years later. This produced, at its best, a somewhat inconsistent form of transportation.

Through the entire trip he kept pumping himself up for the task ahead. He felt totally confident in his ability to fool those he was about to meet, as well as he had taken in everyone in Cork.

'I was a winner in Cork, and I will be an even bigger winner in Dublin.'

Dublin was distant from Cork both in length and what mysteries it had in store for Anthony. It was difficult in both the mental transition and the physical voyage. The closer he came to his destination, the greater his spirit was sapped.

Despite his preaching the positive message on the entire trip, the first sight of Dublin left him white-faced and terrified.

Anthony Angus O'Donnell walked off the train and Dublin immediately hit him right in the mouth. The people were walking so fast that he wondered where they were all racing to. They also seemed far better dressed than ordinary people in Cork would dress. But, what perplexed Anthony most of all, was the almost dead expressions on their faces.

Equally puzzling was that he couldn't find a single street sign. He felt a sense of dread that left him feeling shorter, uncertain, full of fears and weak as a newborn.

He and Blake had mapped out how to get from the train station to the college. Even with these most perfect directions, Anthony managed to get lost more than once.

The enormity of the city and the brusqueness of the people heightened the draining of his usual bravado.

At long last he spotted the building that had to be his new residence. He took a deep breath and tried to muster enough energy to slowly push open the wide doors that led indoors.

The most affable of young men greeted him.

"Hey there, I'm Billy McGovern. I'm in my third year here and, believe me, I may work here, but my words about how lucky you are to be in this fine dorm is as true as can be. What's your name?"

"Anthony Donnell."

McGovern shuffled through some sheets and then muttered, "Are you sure you are registered at Botany Bay Dorm? Check your papers, maybe you are at New Square Dorm. We have a Patrick O'Donnell and an Anthony Angus O'Donnell but no Anthony Donnell here."

"People in Ireland always seem to add an 'O' to my name. I guarantee that I am registered here."

"Well that sure is strange."

"A long time ago my father warned me about that kind of thing happening to me just as it did to him. And this isn't the first time I've gone through that confusion. You see, Dad and his family moved to Cork from Bath in England because his father had gotten a job managing a small shipyard in

Cork. The really funny thing about that is that today my father has the same job."

"Well, whatever you say. I'll make certain that all your papers have the 'O' deleted. First let me show you up to your room."

McGovern whisked Anthony up to a small room on the third floor. There were four beds in the room.

The three others he would be sharing these lavish accommodations with were not expected for a few days. Billy promised that by the end of the week the peace and quiet that prevailed at the moment would then be gone for the next ten months.

"But, if you would rather be in a room just for two, I can arrange that."

"No, I'd rather be with more than less. That way I'll get to meet a larger group. I sure am excited about meeting a lot of new people."

And so he sewed his first seed. McGovern would spread the word that he was just a nice kid who was anxious to meet all his new classmates.

"Here's a bit of advice for ya. Don't plan on studying here. The only way to get anything done is to bury oneself in the library. I'm a study freak. So I am in the library every moment I can spare. If ya ever need my help about anything, ya'll find me at a special desk far in the back of the second library floor."

Anthony had found the first of the men he must cultivate and use.

With it came a renewal of his inner spirit. There would be many more to come, but he felt pleased by this very first meeting.

It took Anthony less than two minutes to put his belongings into the bottom drawer of the bureau standing next to his bed. He took advantage of being the first one in the room. He could not deny himself of the pleasure he would derive from being able to look out of the lone window in the room while lying in bed.

But this was not the time for rest. He took off his suit and good shoes and replaced them with his other more ordinary trousers and comfortable shoes. It was time to explore Dublin.

McGovern was back at the front desk. He heard Anthony clomping down the stairs and took out a small map of the city. He held it out to Anthony who grabbed it and smiled as he thanked his lone friend for it.

"How did you know I would need a map?"

"Simple. Though most of our students are from here, the very first thing the others must do is to walk on just about every street in this great city of ours. Today you, like all the others, will get totally lost trying to find out how this city is laid out. And that is the fun of what you are about to do."

McGovern then proceeded to lay out the convoluted way to get to the five most important sites in Dublin.

First, in order of importance he laid out the way to the famed Liffey River which flowed through and around all of Dublin, in the course of which it divides much of the city. Next to come were the four most famed Irish Pubs

"All four offer great beers, but they are as different as can be. The Temple Bar is the most popular pub in all of

Dublin. But I guarantee, despite the great Irish music which blasts away night and day, it is always so crowded you won't like it."

He then went on to tell the history of the Brazen Head Pub which had been in existence since eleven hundred and seventy eight. It was known for its extra large pints.

Billy then noted that one had to have a pint at The Gock since one family had owned that pub since thirteen ninety. Just looking at the architecture of the old building was worth a visit.

"But my favorite is Mrs. Reilly's. It's a lot smaller than the others but it is always a riot of fun when you are there. They have a great motto, 'If you are in the mood or the ale drives you into a wild jig, just jump on the bar and have at it.' If you are half good, Maura Reilly will be up there with you jigging away. And, when you get there, throw one down for me."

"Well, promise you won't tell anybody, but I have some crazy disease that even if I have just a pint I could chance starting a war in my stomach that just about kills me. So all I can do in a pub is to pitch darts."

"Oh, no, ya are a poor bastard. Are ya sure you're Irish?"

"As a matter of fact, I'm not. I was born in Bath, but I've been in Ireland since I was one year old. But in my heart and soul I am Irish and definitely not some bloody Englishman."

It was his so cherished father, in a rare sober moment, who had taught him that valued lesson, 'Take even one sip of alcohol and soon enough you'll surely become a drunken bum like me.'

In Anthony's mind he knew one could never achieve what he was aiming for if he didn't adhere to his father's advice. Keep those words in mind and there would never be any 'next morning' horrors his father always suffered through.

He shrugged off the dire thoughts of his father and pondered the more important question of the moment. Which way should he go to let Dublin quickly confuse and bewilder him?

With that in mind, he ran out into the street. He took a deep breath and turned as he had been directed towards the Liffey River.

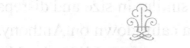

Chapter Twenty Three

Jumping from the pages of the map was a long blue patch that ran through all of Dublin. Obviously it was the famed river, and the first thing he wanted to see. He tried and tried to get close to this great waterway, but the wandering streets of Dublin kept him lost and away from the Liffey.

Looking for street signs was a total loss until he stared up at a triangular shaped building which was at the corner of two streets. Some fifteen feet up, the words 'McDougal Street' were carved into one side of the triangle, while the other side had the words 'MacClagen Street' carved into it.

The magnet of the Liffey forced him to quicken his pace from street to street. It was not too long before he realized that this fervor to find the river was prompted by his being alone, frightened, and more than a little homesick for the waters of Cork. Fortunately, a familiar smell took charge of his walk. It was the odor that also dominated Cork.

Somewhere to the left of him there had to be a big body of water. It must be the Liffey, passing through the city it had conquered. The odor and the dampness grew stronger and, with a sharp left turn, there she was.

With his first sight of the Liffey, a peace descended on Anthony. He soon was walking on the boardwalks that embraced each side of her.

Though most of the boats were far bigger than those in Cork, there were many similar in size and disrepair to those in Cork. It all brought a calm down on Anthony.

As he looked outward upon the Liffey, he felt comforted by the familiarity of this powerful river. He felt the joy that this great city would bring him.

Further down, he could see where the Liffey entered the Irish Sea. Also dominating his eyes was the hustle and bustle of all the people working the river. And in the middle of this wide river there was the same peace that at times dominated the waters of Cork.

He imagined himself setting off on a wonderful craft sailing against the current. Not the dinky rowboats he stole for a quick tour of the sea but a large wind-driven sailboat.

He had conquered Cork and now he would conquer Dublin.

He went back to the directions that Billy had given him to get him to the Temple Bar, and after quite a spell of missteps, he came face to face with what was purported to be the finest pub in the world.

He poked his head in and quickly saw that McGovern was right. It might not be the finest pub, but it certainly was the most crowded pub he had ever seen. It was jammed from the entrance way to as far back as he could see.

An enormous mass of people, mostly of his own age, or a bit older, seemed to cover every square inch of space, and everyone was screaming about a darts game or singing some off-color song about being young and sexually unsatisfied.

This was certainly not the place nor the time to be introducing himself to his fellow students. He did not try to enter but quickly turned away from its entrance.

Instead, he wandered through each street and played the game of trying to memorize each posted name and the shops on each corner of the street. He wrote the info right on the map.

The one thing that seemed familiar to Anthony was the seriousness and the blankness which dominated all that he passed. The Irish Famine was felt even in this big city.

As he strolled along he could not help but look into the faces of the people, all of whom seemed to be racing by him. He saw very few smiles. There were not many people out enjoying the pleasant day and even fewer gossiping with one another.

Dublin was suffering badly but he wanted to shout out, 'Hey what the devil are you crying about? If you think things are tough here, move to Cork. That is Hell and Dublin is Heaven.'

With a smile he continued again on his first tour of Dublin but, to his chagrin, he never did find the Brazen Head nor the ancient Gock.

Chapter Twenty Four

After an hour of touring the city he spotted a sign emblazoned atop the front door of what was obviously a pub. The sign, colored a brilliant gold, read Reilly's and beneath that were the simple words, YOUR PUB.

His thirst and the signage drew Anthony inward. The bar was busy but not frenetic. If anything, it had a welcoming feel of ease and comfort. From behind the bar several men and one, a rather good looking woman, were dolling out the beers and a constant flow of talk.

It was the woman who finally greeted him with. "What will it be young fellow?"

"A pint of your finest please."

"This must be your first time in my establishment if you don't know everything we serve is the finest. So I'll give you a bit of three different ales and you pick out which you most favor."

Sipping from each glass showed him that each had a different taste but all were equally fine. But the finest of all was this handsome lady who kept staring at him from across the bar.

He stretched his hand and said, "I'm Anthony Donnell, and you are right. They are all as great as can be. And, it is also a pleasure to be looking at such a lovely as you are."

"I'm Maura Reilly, the owner of the place. Thanks for the nice words."

With that she grasped his hand and squeezed it tightly. She did so while studying this handsome bird in front of her. She liked what she saw.

The ale was ignored but the eyes clung to each other as strongly as the fingers did.

Finally it was time to break this quiet, but warm tête-à-tête, and Mrs. Reilly slowly eased her hand out of his firm grip.

"Now young man, let me enlighten you about Reilly's. There is a Mr. Reilly and my Patrick looked so much like you when he was your age that I nearly fainted when I saw you come in."

"I'll accept that as a big compliment."

"You got that right my young friend. My husband is as wonderful a man that has ever lived. You walked in, and I knew right off that I had to find out more about you. And, as far as your dreams about how much fun you would have jumping into bed with me, forget it. That will never happen. If you'd like, I'll get you the fairest of Irish maidens to satisfy your need for that sort of thing."

Back in Cork he had his way with many a young damsel but, as to be expected, both he and his bed partners were quite young and totally inexperienced. He had quickly formed visions of learning from Mrs. Reilly as she taught him the correct way to perform those pleasurable acts. Those thoughts quickly disappeared.

"Consider such thoughts totally forgotten. I, like you, know there are a lot more important things for me to concentrate on, and you will be telling me what those are before our chat is over."

"Damn it, I was right. There is a brain behind that handsome face of yours. You are right. I have one helluva lot to tell you. I've got some others to tend to, so drink up and relax, and I'll return in about five."

The five stretched into twenty but she returned, pint in hand, spouting a mass of words which Anthony heard as "Shut your mouth and listen up real good."

She focused on the story of Patrick and Maura buying a down-trodden pub and building it into one of the most successful such places in all of Dublin.

"Hell, our lunch and dinner business brings in a mint. If you add the booze to that, you will see we are doing real well."

She let that sink in while she watched every movement of his face. Her tale had him hooked.

"Now here's the part that may interest you. Patty, Patrick to you, just hated what had happened in this mad country of ours. He tried to fight off that loathing but, three months ago, he left Dublin for New York City. He is working as hard as he can to set something up there that is similar to what we have here."

She paused to quench her thirst. It was water not beer that she drank.

"When he finds the right place for us, we will either sell this place or hire somebody to run it for us and not steal us blind. That's my job. To find the right people to take over Mrs. Reilly's Pub."

"And for what purpose could you be telling me, an eighteen year old, all of that?"

"I have a feeling that somewhere in that brain of yours, there lives a young man who knows how to get people to do what he wants to do. Am I right about that?"

"Lady, you don't know how right you are, but I still don't understand why you are telling me all of this."

"Because that is what is needed to make a place like this successful. If I am right, and it won't take me long to see who and what you really are, I'll be hailing your success. If I am wrong, I'll be berating myself for so badly misreading you."

"Wait a second. Are you saying you want me to take over Mrs. Reilly's Pub? Are you crazy? I'm just a kid from Cork, and if you don't think my head is turning upside down this very second, then you are a bigger dreamer than I am. I'm in Dublin to get an education at Trinity."

"Of course you are, and, no, I don't expect you to be the head man. I do believe there are others you may know who are of the correct age range and possibly have a large sum of quid in their pockets. To be honest, I have yet to find anyone to fit what I have in mind. That is why I speak to everyone including an eighteen year old college freshman."

Instantly the thought that this place could be bought for relatively little money popped into his mind. Steve, or his brothers, would have the money, and be more than willing to be the backers.

"There might be someone such as you describe."

"Good. Then let me go on. I know I am the best person to teach you and your associates what it takes to run this place. With the proper training, you and your backers could

109

do a grand job here. All I am asking now is for you to come on board. It won't take long for me to either fire your ass, or we will both be smiling at how my instincts never fail."

"Mrs. Reilly, I have been in Dublin for less than a day. I don't know what classes I'll be taking, and I don't know how to pour a beer into a glass and not the countertop. So all that I am hearing sounds like a lot of nonsense to me."

"Yes, I am sure it does, but if you factor in how wise I am, and the fact that I will personally teach you how to make Dublin and Trinity work for you, it might just make a lot of sense. Does any part of that interest you?"

She kept her eyes directed at this fresh young man as she let those words sink in

Anthony frowned at first, but then the temptation of what she was saying began to pick at him.

"May I repeat, I'm just a dumb kid who is hearing a beautiful woman speak words that don't make any sense to him, and you expect an intelligent answer now?"

"No way, take a day or a week or never come back. I'll be looking forward to seeing you again my young friend, either as someone needing a beer or a fellow who is willing to gamble on being a winner. Finish your lager, and I'll give you another, and both will be on the house."

He then repeated almost word for word what he told Mike about his beer consumption.

"But I'll accept your offer for the one I am about to finish."

"That makes you even more worthy of being considered for the job."

Anthony kept his focus on the woman's eyes, and she stayed right there with him.

He took one large swig of the ale then turned to go. Before reaching the front door he looked back and, of course, there she stood looking at him. He threw her a silent kiss and got one back in kind.

He had made an important friend.

Chapter Twenty Five

He almost ran in his haste to get back to the Liffey. The smell of fresh sea water and the constant waterfront activity was what he was craving. He desperately needed a place where he could feel at home, and right at this moment, the Liffey was the only place that could give him the ease to think about all the craziness he had just heard.

'Of course I would be a great success with Mrs. Reilly leading the way. Are you crazy? You need help to just tie your shoe laces. And school? There is no way you are going to drop the much needed schooling and become a bartender. You are an idiot. Why the hell are you even thinking about this stupidity?'

Back and forth he flowed. First, being avidly against her ideas, and then wanting to give it a try. Maybe going along with her was the path to the success he yearned for. Or would that route, with easy access to all the beer he wanted, lead him to being like his father, a drunken bum?

People passing him on the street were jolted as this nice looking young man suddenly began screaming out, "Oh no. Not me, not ever me."

Sharing a single beer with Mrs. Reilly would be a pure and simple act, but more appealing would be the other offerings she had proposed. Certainly Mrs. Reilly's younger friends would be most exciting and fill in a blank in his worldliness. But he really was most enthused about the lessons that would be forthcoming from the 'grand dame' herself. He looked forward to being a very good student.

After a harried hour, he made a turn away from the waters and started racing back to Maura's pub. It was time to start class.

Chapter Twenty Six

If anything, the bar was even more crowded than when he had left her but two hours ago. What was missing was the one person he had come to see. No matter how hard he looked, there was not a sight of Maura Reilly.

He finally elbowed his way up to the bar and caught the eye of a bartender.

The expected, "What'll it be?" came forth and same was answered with, "I'm Anthony Donnell, and I have to get a message through to Mrs. Reilly. Is she here?"

"I'll be seeing if she is available."

Of course the bartender first went to the office where he knew he would find the lady in question.

"So, he came back quicker than I thought. Danny, ignore him for the next fifteen minutes and then give him a lager and bring him back here. And, Mike, spread the word that I want everyone to give him a good look, and I want to be told whenever he shows up here. He may be the answer to one of our problems."

It was closer to twenty minutes later when Danny found the time to pour a lager for Anthony.

"Just go to the far end of the bar. I'll meet you there and take you to Mrs. Reilly's office. Here are a couple of lagers for you and the good Mrs."

It took some heavy pushing and many 'Pardon me's' before Anthony got to their meeting place.

Spinning away from Anthony, Danny muttered, "You're sure not a swift one is ya? Knock on that second door down the hall and she'll be calling ya in."

And with that Mike strode away.

It took four knocks before Anthony heard, "Don't be breaking my door you daft kid. Now come on in."

It was awkward holding on to the two beers and opening the door, but he managed to get in without too much spillage.

"Well this is a surprise visit. You sure didn't see much of our city now did you?"

"I saw plenty, but the more I saw, the more I heard you saying how you were willing to teach me of Dublin and Trinity. So, I thought, why not start right away."

Maura Reilly took the glass of lager he had brought to her and lifted it in toast to Anthony.

"Welcome back."

Anthony did not lift his glass in reply.

"You are too smart to have forgotten what I said about my beer drinking. So you are obviously either testing me or playing a game with me. I suggest you don't do either. I am the most serious eighteen year old you have ever met."

The rebuke did not phase the lady one bit. His speedy return had confirmed in her mind that this young man was the right man for the job she had in mind.

"I apologize. You are right. I was testing you. That will never happen again. What I will promise you is that if this deal of ours does work out, I will teach you more than you could ever learn from a thousand professors. But the deal falls apart if you don't earn a degree from Trinity. Between me and your schooling, you're going to be one ultra successful young man."

My God, she had just uttered his favorite word. His head was ablaze with pride, but he wisely contained his reply to a simple 'thank you' and then continued on by telling her of what he had gone through for the past hours.

"All the conflicting thoughts nearly drove me mad. But I did accomplish one thing. I made up my mind. I want to start my lessons right now."

"No, no. There won't be any teachings tonight. Don't be looking so downcast. You'll be getting a ton of lessons from me in due time. But what I will give you now, and in much detail, is more information for you to dwell on. Then I'm going to throw you out of here until you can give me an answer to a question I will lay before you."

Once again she launched into a long description about her wonderful husband and their mutual plans. She then started on about how she would personally train Anthony in how to successfully run a pub.

"And, everyone who works here calls me 'Maura.'"

"Thank you, Maura, and now can I give you some more about me. Once you have told me something, you never have to repeat it to me. But now I will repeat something to you. I am very interested in what you have proposed. And I do have an older friend from Cork who has the money to buy this place."

"Good enough. But I don't like quick decisions. I don't want to see you again for at least a month, or however long it takes you to feel at ease about how you're handling your school work and if there is room in your life to take a job here as well. That's my question and it isn't an easy one to answer."

He added one sentence. "I'll be back in one month."

Chapter Twenty Seven

During the rest of the month, he never entered any pub, nor downed a beer. He went into training to be the best student ever to darken Trinity's halls and to prove to Maura that taking over her business would be well within his capabilities

Nothing at school fazed him. In fact he felt that most of his fellow students were nowhere near him in his intensive desire to learn, learn and learn. And learn he did.

His enormous ego responded accordingly. Here he was this kid from Cork already standing out in school, and an outrageous lady had seen something of value in him, offering him, a first year college student, the opportunity of a lifetime.

All of it, of course, was how Steve would react to this crazed offer.

How should he make his presentation to Steve? A raft of devious approaches flew through his mind, and then one plan wakened him to the easiest and most worthwhile approach. Just tell him the truth.

Within moments he had penned a brief note. The entire message contained two short sentences reading, 'You must come to Dublin immediately. Something amazing has been offered to me, and I need you to help me make a decision.'

Its reply was equally brief.

'Thank you for your most totally non-informative letter. Despite my first thought that you are absolutely balmy, I shall arrive next Saturday with all the answers you need.'

To be certain that he was at the station when Steve arrived, Anthony was there at nine A.M. Steve got off the first train from Cork at two P.M. The hug they shared was a delight for both men.

Halfway to Anthony's room he had told Steve everything about the amazing Maura and the incredible offer she had laid at their feet. Anthony emphasized the word 'their' as he kept saying this could be great for both of them.

"Anthony, you were correct in asking that I help you in making the decision. I want you to introduce me to that lady and then not to say another word while she and I talk. What you and I will do is to hear her out, and then I will tell her that I must talk to my brothers, who, I am certain, have the monies needed and are well versed in business machinations. Do you agree to that?"

Anthony merely nodded his head not wanting to cause any dissension but not liking the role assigned to him in the meeting with Maura

An hour later they were seated in Maura's office sipping a fine lager and listening intently as she, in some detail, explained what she had in mind.

"Mrs. Reilly, I must say it sounds like a good offer. But no, I cannot give you any more of a response. First off, I am merely a poor teacher and don't have the foggiest notion about business. Anthony may think I am wise about all, but take me away from books, and I am as ill-prepared to give you an intelligent offer as he is. What I can tell you is that there is no way that I would allow Anthony to leave school for all the fortunes of the world."

"I am in total accord with you on that, but I have no doubt that he can handle school and a part time job here."

"Good. Then I must get my brothers to come here to meet with you. You will enjoy them. They are very successful business men, and I am certain they will have many questions to ask of you."

"That sounds fine to me."

He then asked her for a fiscal accounting of her business for the past three years.

"Not a problem. We each have the same need of others to make a decision. You need your brothers, and I cannot make a final decision without my husband's approval. It will probably take some time to put that all together. Why don't I contact him and then advise you of when he can be here."

Anthony, who had been nothing more than an observer for the entire discussion, knew only that all was going on far too slowly for his tastes. He was eager to push the deal-making forward.

"I think that we should...."

"No, Anthony, Mrs. Reilly has offered a fair plan."

Without a beat, a date was set for all parties to meet in Dublin towards the middle of the next month.

"Well how about my starting to work for you now?"

Both Blake and Maura quickly cut off that idea with the firm announcement that Anthony's only job at this moment was to see if he could adjust to college activities, not the bar. Nothing could infringe on that task.

Chapter Twenty Eight

School posed only one annoyance to Anthony. The freshman class, with its large group of unsophisticated young boys, stood awkwardly apart from the more seasoned young men who had already spent one to three years at the school.

It wasn't long before each of the sophomores made the worthless freshmen understand their ranking in the school. It was the remembrance of what they had endured the preceding year that spurred their loathing for their inferiors. Their intensity reached incredible heights of cruelty.

The older students were also demeaning of the new group of worthless beings but nothing as compared to the sophomores.

Steve Blake had previously advised Anthony of the ignominy that awaited him. He warned his young ward about not getting upset by that nonsense and that all would pass away soon enough. Because of Steve's warning, Anthony took the casual commands and demands rather easily.

Yes, he would shine their shoes or search for a too hard to find library book. Somehow or other, the book could never be found, which, of course, led to other horrors being presented to the brainless freshmen.

One was the wearing of an ultra large badge that proclaimed him to be a worthless freshman. It also carried the message to call this asshole of a sub-human, 'Tony, the Idiot.'

He would gratefully sing the school song while dancing a jig. He would do anything requested of him, no matter how silly and humiliating it was. No problem, as long as he could laugh at himself and the stupidity of the tasks he was asked to perform. But one particularly vengeful lad went too far for Anthony's taste.

He had asked Anthony to drop down to the pub and buy some beers for a group of sophomores. Anthony said he would gladly do so, but would they give him the money for the beers first?

"How dare you ask for money? Just get your dumb ass down there and tell them who the beers are for."

And with that remark he hauled off and landed a solid kick on Anthony's backside. This brought a great roar of laughter from the three others in the room.

Anthony wasted not a moment. He grabbed the kicker by his collar, lifted him in the air and fiercely shook him. He then threw him to the floor.

"You ever raise a hand or foot to me again, and I'll break every bone in your body. And, if any of the rest of you would like to try something like that, let's get on with it right now."

Not one of the three moved an inch forward.

News of the event soared through the school, and all sorts of plans were laid to teach Anthony a lesson or two. A few of the more aggressive ones even tried to implement their moves against him. Only one such attempt was actually initiated, but the pain they suffered at Anthony's hands far surpassed anything he felt.

Word spread that he would gladly do any ridiculous request with a smile, but go beyond that, and you will learn not to tempt fate. If anything, his attitude brought him great respect from most of the student body. He had quickly shown how a leader acted. There was no doubt but who the leader in this great school would eventually be.

Anthony quickly recognized his new position and loved every minute of it. He realized that his credo of the necessity to succeed had once again been realized. But he did not enjoy what brought him this success. To succeed by violence demeaned the power of the mind, and that was where his real strength must shine.

People knew him because of his strength, but his task was now to convert that to people being envious of his mind. The planning was pure Anthony.

He walked up to Michael McGuire, the very tall and handsome senior class president, as he was leaving an early morning class.

"Mr. McGuire, could I possibly have a word with you, sir?"

McGuire stared down at his questioner. This was not easy as Anthony had grown to be over six feet tall. McGuire of course had heard of the rogue freshman.

"And who the hell are you?"

"I'm Anthony Donnell and I'm a freshman here, and I need your advice, sir"

"Well I've got a meeting to go to, but walk with me and ask away."

In his research about McGuire, Anthony had discovered the senior was considered to be a near genius in Advanced Arithmetic. The question he posed was to evoke serious interest upon McGuire's part.

"Actually, it is a two-part question. First off, I have an arithmetic problem that I have encountered. I really love problems like that, but I seem to always be fighting off most of the student body, so I have no time to do what I most want to be doing."

"Well what the hell has that to do with me?"

"I would like to offer you my services for anything you need and, in return, I would be able to tell all those hooligans that I only work for you. That will scare them off and, I am certain, that will end all the fights and allow me to get to do what I really love which is arithmetic."

McGuire stopped in his tracks. He did not say a word to Anthony but just kept looking at him. He then started to walk away with Anthony trailing him.

"You really don't have an arithmetic problem do you?"

"Of course not. I just said that so you might consider I was worth talking to."

"Why did you think that?"

"Because I have something I want to offer you."

"What would you do if I just bashed in that loud mouth of yours?"

"I'd just bash you back, and then we would have one great fight. After that I would repeat my offer to serve you."

"You know, you are one ballsy freshman."

"Yes, sir, I do know that."

"And what you really want is having me protect you from all that fighting."

"No, sir, I can easily handle all of the fighting. What I really want is the freedom of time to do what I want to do and whatever you want me to do."

"Donnell, you are a joke, but I must commend you for coming up with this grand scam. You're on. Meet me at my room in a couple of hours and we will see if all your shite is worthy of my attention.

Anthony won his first step upwards. He would make certain that he would be more than valuable to McGuire.

In time, what was a boy and his boss became a true friendship of almost equals.

The result of this friendship brought equal gains for both. McGuire found that Donnell was quick and decisive in fulfilling every request tended to him. More and more the requests became increasingly demanding. In return the relationship became almost equal in importance between the asker and the doer.

McGuire's rein as head of the student body was esteemed by all the student body and many of the faculty. That kid, Donnell, was soon recognized as being a remarkably bright freshman and one who was to be closely watched.

It wasn't long before the matters they discussed with each other became of graver matter. Within the very first month of Anthony's servitude, a subject arose that changed all in his life.

It started late one night when each of them was sipping their first and last beer of the night. Anthony had found great favor with McGuire when he revealed that he too limited his beer drinking to one a day. And when the reason why he limited his consumption emerged, McGuire almost screamed with delight.

It seemed that each of their fathers were similar. The only difference was that one was wealthy and a drunken bum and the other was poor and a drunken bum.

"Why did your father, with all his money, go that way?"

"It was because of the money that he drank. He battled all day to get richer and richer and nothing else in his life mattered. I guess he drank to keep his sanity."

On hearing that Anthony roared with laughter,

"Hey you little twit that's not a laughing matter!"

"I'm not laughing at your father. I'm laughing at my father because he kept at the beer kegs because he didn't have a quid, and he never found any way to get any. I guess he too drank to keep his sanity."

Their mutual laughter finally led Anthony to inquire how McGuire hoped to stay a one-beer-a-day drinker when he left school and joined the business world.

"Where the hell did you get the idea that I would follow that drunk in his lust for money? Not a chance. You think I want to become what my father is? Let me tell you something. I love being the leader of all the dummies in this class. I love the power and I love that everyone goes out of their way to kiss my bottom."

"Hey, I sure know what you are talking about, and I also know that your need to be the leader won't end when you leave college. Come on, what do you intend to do?"

"I'll tell you what. Hopefully I should be getting word about something I have been working on for over a year now. I'll tell you all about it if the answer is what I want it to be. So, for the present, keep your fat mouth shut as to what you may or may not think."

That conversation engendered a new thought for Anthony to ponder over. Could it be the fact that Mike's father had bequeathed so much money to Mike that he just had no need for more? Or could it be that money itself brought with it so many complications as to foul up ones real yearnings?

All of which led to the question, *'Was Maura's bar worth the effort if its only reward was the accumulation of money and all its attendant woes?'*

Chapter Twenty Nine

Anthony was ever diligent about what had made Mike McGuire so powerful. His admiration for the school leader pushed him into learning everything his 'boss' had done in his almost four years at Trinity.

One fact he uncovered really stunned him. McGuire had taken every theological course available.

What most puzzled him was that McGuire never went to church and never discussed religion with anyone. Why all the preoccupation with what had to be the dullest classes in the school? His major had been mathematics, but he could surely have graduated with a degree in religion.

One of Anthony's daily tasks was to gather the mail McGuire got each day. He was further confused when he realized that a good deal of the mail came from seminaries in England.

"Mike, can I ask you a personal question?"

"No you can't, but somehow you will wiggle an answer out of me. So, go ahead and ask the question. Whether or not you get an answer depends on what I think you should know or not know."

Those words were not the words Anthony hoped to hear. He nodded slowly while waving the mail at McGuire as if it was a baton.

"Okay, we'll play it your way. No questions asked, and no answers needed.

Instead, Anthony slyly laid out what he really wanted to know.

"You know I believe that most people are total asses who need to be led. I think you believe so as well.

"You stun me with your astuteness. Come on my under nourished young friend. What is it that you really want to say?"

In response, a torrent of thoughts poured out. It covered Mike being a natural leader and loving that role. This was followed by his confession about wanting to be a leader as well.

"Hey logger-head, did you think that I didn't already know that?"

"How would you know that?"

"Every time we come across some stupid junior or senior, I see your eyes start to boil. At times, I think I am the only one in this entire school that you admire, and sometimes I wonder if I'm not included in that stupid group."

"That's nonsense. You are my hero. What I most want is for you to get me on the path you've paved. I am trying to learn everything about you. I study everything you do. You don't want me to probe into your private doings, okay, that's fine with me. But, please explain one crazy thing to me."

"Sure, I'll explain away, but don't expect to get an honest answer."

"Fine, I know you have taken, or will be taking every religious course available in this school. Your mail, just like today, is always filled with letters from seminaries all over England. So, what the hell is that all about?"

At that Mike jumped up and grabbed Anthony. McGuire's face had turned beet red following Anthony's last words.

"You little wart, I am going to give you one minute to get out of this room before I beat the devil out of you."

"No, beat away, but before we start this battle hear me out. You don't have to tell me anything."

"You are beyond being a stupid nosy beast. Why the hell should I let you into any of my private doings or thoughts?"

"Because, I really need to keep you as my friend. You are the one real friend I have in this entire town."

Mike loosened his grip on Anthony, but the anger still lingered in his face.

"Come on, you know that we share a dream! You want to be very successful. I want to win every battle I encounter. You will do anything to get to the top, and I am right there with you

"Hey, the very first time you approached me, I knew that you were cursed with the same urges that plagued me. But I still don't see that as a reason to tell you one blamed thing about me. I will give you one piece of advice. You don't know shite about the real world. You don't have an inkling of an idea about the business world and I'm absolutely certain that the church world is equally foreign to you."

"Before you throw me out of here, can I tell you something that is very important to me and ask your advice about it?"

"What the hell could you tell me that would interest me?"

Desperate not to lose Mike's friendship Anthony spelled out the ongoing discussions with Maura Reilly.

Mike quickly cooled down.

"Now, that is really interesting. What do I think about it? Grab it. It could be great for you."

"Are you still my friend?"

"Maybe so, but without answers to your questions. So here is what I will tell you. Before you leave these hallowed quarters, get your brain working and find out what makes the business world and the church world tick. Get off your fat backside and learn about both of them. Now get out of my sight before I really get sick of you."

Anthony was about to reply but a further look at McGuire sent off a menacing message. Get out of the room before McGuire throws you out via the double window in his room.

Halfway out the door, he stopped and turned back to a man who was but a few years older but was light years wiser.

"Mike, can I tell you one more terrible thing. I come from the worst background one could imagine. Because of that, I have made a pact with the devil. I will do anything, hurt and rob anyone. I will do that because if I don't succeed, I will kill myself. Can you understand that?"

"I know everything that you think is hidden within you. I pity you and I pray that you will change, but I doubt if you ever will. I will always be here for you. I will always be your friend. Maybe we will both be lucky and not hurt too many people in the years to come."

Now there were two men in the world, Steve Blake and Mike McGuire that Anthony could believe in and learn from.

Chapter Thirty

With things in school going just fine and with Mike's now constant tutoring, Anthony felt at ease to think again about Maura's proposition concerning Mrs. Reilly's Pub.

Steve Blake had forwarded to his brothers all the information Maura had given him. She, in turn, had written to her husband. As promised, Anthony had stayed away from the pub, but now knew he had to push both sides to pick up the pace.

He had written Steve and the return message said his brothers would be in Dublin as soon as the other side was ready.

Getting to Maura was easy enough. Large smiles from each of the barmen greeted his entrance into the pub. A big hug from Maura made all well for him.

"Your timing is perfect. I just got word from my husband that he will be here within the next week or so. What is new on your side?"

"Steve Blake told me that they will be here as soon as your husband arrives. So I'll tell him to be in Dublin at the end of next week."

"Anthony, I am certain all of this is going to work out just fine."

"So am I, but more to the point I have a favor to ask of you. I want to start working here as soon as you will let me."

Anthony's emphatically voiced tone provoked the exact answer he had not expected to receive.

"Not a chance, my young friend. The more I thought about our deal the more I knew that you need at least a half a year before you are in any way distracted from your school work."

Once again, be it any of the three people he most admired, Steve, Mike or Maura, he was always getting turned down in what he wanted. He knew that he had school well in hand, but here was Maura saying he was wrong.

He knew he was ready to handle any learning chances, be it school or bar. This turn-down of what he knew he could do greatly bothered him.

"Why can't I get anybody to tell me that I know what I want, and I know what I am doing?"

"Oh, I am sure you know what you want, but that doesn't mean you have to get everyone to immediately bow to your wishes, Besides that, I promise you whether or not our deal goes through, you'll be working here soon enough."

He knew he was dead in this battle. Nothing would change her opinion.

Chapter Thirty One

Later that week Steve Blake arrived in Dublin with news that his brothers would be there the next day.

Anthony invited Mike to have dinner with him and his special friend, Steve. He didn't say a single word to Mike about Steve's sexual preferences. Nor was it brought up for the entire evening.

"I've taken you here, to Reilly's Pub, for three reasons. First, I assure you that Maura, the owner of this place, won't have any bill tendered to us. Secondly, you will adore her, despite the fact that she is the meanest, ugliest, grouchiest person who ever owned a pub. And the third reason is that despite her appearance, she has the good sense to stock the best beers you will ever taste."

Steve jumped in with an in depth review of the possible forthcoming purchase of the pub.

"Well, if all falls apart because of something you or your brothers are not happy with, I am sure my father knows more than one man or two who would love to take on this enterprise."

Mike lifted his glass and took a big slug of ale when Maura noticed them and came to their table.

"Well look who deigned to honor my little pub."

A gush of beer spewed out from Mike's mouth and the remainder of the beer poured out of the large bottle he also knocked over. It was as if he had suffered some catatonic fit.

Fittingly he managed to squeeze out "I am so sorry."

"Maura, please excuse Mike. His friend, young Anthony, who is known far and wide as an inveterate liar, has just described you in terms that weren't quite accurate, so that when you appeared Mike was more than shaken by the real you."

Slightly recovered, Mike strongly shouted "Mrs. Reilly, that devil of an oaf told me you were mean, ugly and grouchy."

"Well Anthony correctly described me. Could you now tell me what caused the eruption that caused the wastage of some fine ale?"

In response the three gentlemen, as one, rose and pulled out a chair so that Maura could join them.

"Well I think the best thing I can do to end this catastrophe is to just admit I am an oaf and the liar Steve claimed I was. I apologize to all of you."

Steve broke the hilarious laughter that engulfed all when he raised his glass and offered a toast to Maura. "Mrs. Reilly, may all your wishes be fulfilled by the end of this week."

"I hope that my husband and Steve's brothers find a way to make this all happen. And, gentlemen my name is 'Maura' so please drop the stuffy, 'Mrs. Reilly.'"

"Well, Maura, can I start our relationship by asking if I then agreed to only call you Maura and then ask Maura if I could join Anthony in working for her?

"If I am correct in believing that you are a junior or a senior then the answer is, 'yes.' I am not sure of the 'when,' but it will be shortly."

The packed house soon drew her back to work but with a promise to rejoin them as soon as possible. "And there will be no check, but make sure you take good care of your server."

Chapter Thirty Two

On their way home, Steve laughingly told Mike and Anthony that he was heading for a bar he knew of that catered to men like himself.

"And if I ever learn of either of you going there, I will personally whip you to death.

Of course as soon as he turned away, Anthony had to explain that statement.

"But, bottom line, I more than like him. He is a good guy who has been like a real father to me. Considering what a louse I was to him when we first met, there is no better man in the world than Steve Blake."

Anthony went on to tell Mike in lurid detail what he had done to Steve. "But when I really needed help, I ran to him, and he saved my life."

The discussion of Steve lasted until they reached Mike's dorm.

The seriousness with which Anthony explained it all allowed Mike to add another dimension to their talk.

"Tell me something. Do you really want to limit yourself to being the owner of a Dublin pub? There is a hell of a lot more waiting for you than that."

"Mike that is the first really stupid remark I have ever heard you mutter. You, Mr. Son of a Rich Man, don't have to worry about money while I, the son of a man without a farthing, worry about money all the time."

"Grow up, and stop wailing at the world about all your troubles. It isn't money that is your problem. It is your belief that you are a lesser man than me and, God knows, how many others. Now, get your sorry ass out of my room before I throw you out head first."

Beyond furious, Anthony flew from Mike's room. He slammed his own door so hard that his roommates, who usually could sleep through anything, jumped out of bed each screaming away at the earthquake that had just hit their room.

"Shut your faces and your mouths, or I will beat you 'til I've knocked all the blood out of you."

One look at Anthony and the covers were drawn over every inch of their bodies. Sleep came slowly, but it finally came and brought with it a gentle peace.

It was otherwise for Anthony. He had never been so angry. Questions about Mike and himself kept battling in his mind.

How dare Mike scoff at my needs? What the hell did he know about what happens to a person who has to count every quid he has?

Two questions tore a bit of the anger away from Anthony and led him into deeper thought about the pub.

The first was simple enough. What's wrong with owning a pub anyway?

But by far the most self-troubling question claimed possession of Anthony.

What did he mean when he said I thought I was a lesser man? He's crazy. I am the best. Definitely he is crazy. Or is he right? Is all my palaver about being great just a ton of nonsense? Look what I've already proven. I know I can and will get much further. Am I scared of being a failure? Am I jumping at the pub because I really don't have the strength to do any better than that?

There was little sleep for Anthony that night. He groggily awoke early the next morning with one final question.

Could Mike be correct in his assessment of me? Should I give more thought to where I am going? And where the hell is that?

Chapter Thirty Three

The resolution of the sale of the Reilly's Pub could not have gone easier. Truth be told, it was a pact made in heaven. Both sides were eager to make the deal.

The fact of the matter is that merely two hours of face to face negotiation led to the agreement to let each side take one full day of private deliberations to determine whether they were happy enough to make the deal.

Each side knew that Maura's astoundingly handsome husband, Patrick, was on the verge of closing the negotiations for a bar in a very Irish neighborhood in New York City.

But, of those seated in Maura's office only she and Patrick knew that if they couldn't, within the next week or two, come up with all the money needed, their deal in New York would fall apart.

Accordingly, Maura and Patrick lowered the price they had initially proffered.

Actually, the lower price still gave them enough cash to easily complete their New York transition. It also left them enough working capital to make the changes they wanted to make 'Reilly's New York' sing.

Mike's father had been invited to join the purchasing, but he had turned down the opportunity.

As he told Mike, "It sounds like a good opportunity for a young couple or any number of others but we should not be dabbling in this small potatoes sort of business. It could do nothing but diminish our reputation as astute business men. So we will pass on this."

Steve's brothers were rather pleased at the position he had taken as they felt they were stealing the business. Without any dispute, Steve was named the on-site manager.

It was an idea that delighted Steve, as he was more than willing to do so for a period of time while he tried to find a way to get on the faculty of Trinity College.

Of course, Anthony and Mike were soon hired to work weekends. Anthony was most anxious to take over Steve's chores, but Mike said his tenure at the pub depended on whether or not certain plans of his came through.

Maura would stay at the pub for three months and then hie off to America.

"You will be amazed at how little it takes to keep everyone happy about coming here for their bit of ham and ale. You will learn every trick in the trade about what you must do to continue this pub being as successful as it is now."

Their working together brought Mike and Anthony even closer. At school Mike was still the boss, but being co-workers at the pub tightened their friendship. If anything, they became like brothers, but Mike was always the older brother and Anthony the almost as smart younger brother.

One late Saturday night, Mike turned to Anthony and told him of a great letter that had just been sent to his home.

"My father was so excited about it that he came here early this morning and brought me that letter."

The letter advised Mike that he had been accepted into St. Kiernan's College, the oldest and most prestigious Catholic Seminary in Ireland.

With great pride Mike announced, "Anthony this is something I have dreamed of over half of my life. I am going to become a Catholic priest."

Anthony was stunned. He did not know how to respond. The only thing he could force out was a weak 'congratulations' which was followed with, 'But I don't recall you ever going to a church service.'

"You are right. I vowed to myself that if I couldn't be a priest, I didn't want to have anything to do with religion. I wanted to go to the finest Catholic school in the country. And, wonder of wonders, I was just accepted to St. Kiernan's which is the best of the best. It's been around for over one hundred years, and most of the great leaders in the church were students there."

Church meant nothing to Anthony. All it brought to mind was his mother praying to God as she really was worshiping the fine ladies she sat behind in the dingy Cork church near their pitiful home.

"But you are so smart and so strong and you could be a great leader in this country. Why are you settling for something so far behind what you can achieve?"

"But you are wrong my friend. That is just it. I am going to be a strong leader. I am going to spend my life fighting as hard as I can to make everybody's life better. That has been my dream since I was ten years old. Today, Ireland is still suffering from the Potato Famine. Well give me ten years, and we will be fighting our way out of that malaise."

"But, you are almost the most constant exploiter of young women I know of. You have been very good at that game. You are a devoted womanizer. Are you telling me that is over with?"

"Hardly, but, believe me, the day I become a priest that ends."

Anthony's antipathy to all religions brought out angry words that he should not have expressed.

"That is nothing more than you bull shitting yourself. I can't think of a more corrupt body than those thieves who tell us all the time to give them more money, and we will be saved. My mother would steal money from my father so that she would look like some grand lady every Sunday. And, behind her back, they all laughed at her. And, that supposed holy man on the pulpit did nothing but smile at her and join those miserable women in ignoring my simpleton of a mother."

"Anthony, you may have had a bad priest, or maybe it was just your mother who was the culprit trying to steal her way into other people lives. But that is not me. I am going to deliver on everything I say."

"Oh sure, listen to what you just said. First you piss all over a woman you know nothing about, and then you shout about how virtuous a man you are a going to be."

Mike opened his door, pointed his hand outward, and showed Anthony the way to leave.

What had been a grand pact of two soul brothers teetered on the edge of two enemies facing off against one another.

Anthony found not a word to respond. He stood as tall as he could and showed Mike his back as he sauntered out.

All he could think of was…what a loss we are going to suffer. Here was the born leader that Ireland desperately needed and he was going to spend his life under the shelter of a Priest's attire. Anthony almost cried at the waste.

For the remainder of the time Mike had at Trinity they maintained a relationship, but their deep friendship was over. Yes they both worked at the Pub but never on the same shifts.

It wasn't long before Maura sensed there was something amiss between the two, but she was too full of dreams about America to pursue the issue.

Steve knew that a battle had risen between the two. He gave a meager try at getting to the bottom of it but he was too busy learning what it took to replace her and, therefore, walked away from their problems.

With no one available to serve as a peacemaker, the former friends went separate ways.

Mike found another freshman to do his errands and focused on the fulfillment of what had been the dream of almost his entire life.

As for Anthony, he loved who he was and where he was. At the age of eighteen he had put a big business deal together. He was tall, handsome and had a gift for words that all beneath him envied. His sense of self worth kept friends away from him. Few liked him, but all were in awe of him.

There was little doubt but that one day he would be the real replacement for Mike.

His self esteem was tinged with a bit of arrogance that few respected, but that bothered him not one bit. If anything, it further assured him that the coming years would be filled with one success after another.

Chapter Thirty Four

The good Reverend Donnell almost jumped out of his wicker chair. More and more as he aged, his Saturday afternoon retreats would find him asleep and into the midst of some very complex dreams.

What had shaken him out of his torpor this time was the hearty laughter and delighted shouts that accompanied the signing of the papers that transferred the ownership of Mrs. Reilly's Dublin Pub.

Being rudely shaken out of the pleasantest of dreams that he most always adored, forced him into other more recent moments in his life that were far less enjoyable.

That afternoon he had first been dreaming about the glorious days at Trinity and his wonderful coup of breaking precedent by assuming leadership of the student body while just beginning his junior year.

James Burns, soon to be a senior, was the likely winner of that post.

That assumption disappeared when a scurrilous, unsigned letter was circulated. It stated that Burns had raped a young lass who worked in the cafeteria.

Burns denied the allegation vowing that he never spent a moment alone with the girl. She, fighting to keep her job at the school, sided with Burns and kept saying she was still a virgin.

Several members of Burns' class spread the word that she was definitively a liar. On the contrary, she was the easiest lay in town.

Several of the students knew that the girl was a frequenter at the Reilly's Pub, but Anthony was never linked to the girl.

Oddly enough, the young girl and all her friends never paid for their beers at the bar until she was strongly advised by Anthony that she was no longer welcome at the Pub.

The allegation was never proven one way or the other, but it was damaging enough to force Burns to withdraw from the race. His prior record of being highly respected by the student body prevented his being expelled.

Most people questioned the validity of the letter, yet no one wanted to try to take his place. They all feared that they too would be tainted for some equally horrendous act.

Anthony eloquently defended Burns but, though only a junior, he allowed himself to be forced into taking on the leadership role.

Many of his fellow students who were not enamored of Anthony were often heard to mutter that it wouldn't surprise them to learn that the letter was initiated by the only one who benefitted from this dire event.

None of that bothered Anthony who enjoyed every moment of his precedent-breaking two years as the student leader.

Once again he had proven his way was the right way.

Chapter Thirty Five

One of the more glorious events the Reverend Donnell loved to return to was the grand dinner and dance event the faculty hosted for the soon to graduate seniors. Dublin's Dunaway Hotel had been in existence for almost one hundred years and had always hosted this so important event.

Because of the dreadful Irish famine the event had been, for some years now, rather modest in its presentation. But, a little of its famed grandeur seemed to surface for Anthony.

Pleasants Asylum, a woman's school, began its life early in the eighteen hundreds in Dublin as an orphanage. Through the years education became its focus, and its programs of dance, music, art and teaching grew to be known throughout the English speaking world.

Now only very qualified and wealthy young women were admitted to the school. For some time the leading student of Pleasants was invited to be the Mistress of Trinity's dance. Her escort was always the leader of the student body at Trinity. Thus Valerie Ann Morrison got to meet Anthony Angus Donnell.

Anthony's wayward way with women was the talk of Trinity, but after researching Miss Morrison and learning that her father, Mr. Richard Vines Morrison, was one of the wealthiest Englishmen now living in Dublin, he knew that this young lady must be treated in a totally different manner.

He was the handsomest, sweetest and most courteous man she had ever met.

Oh yes, she was quite pretty. She also danced quite well, and they were a handsome couple as they swept through dance after dance.

He took her home after the big party and asked if she would allow him to ask her parents if he might call on her. She was jubilant in his desire to get to know her better.

The night he made his call, her father was away on business, but Anthony charmed Mrs. Morrison, and she, gushingly, approved his coming by the house whenever he could.

Midway in their talk, Mrs. Morrison asked Valerie if she could go up to her room and get her a clean kerchief.

"This will accomplish two purposes. One my nose won't go dripping down my cheek and, secondly, it will give me a minute or two alone with this very nice young man."

As Valerie approached the door, her mother gave the final admonishment to take her time on returning.

"I very much adore that girl and her father does as well. But I must tell you something very disturbing about my husband. May I do so without your saying a word of it to Valerie?"

"You have my word on it."

Mrs. Morrison blew her nose much more than was needed before she spoke again.

"My husband can be terrible to anyone who is not one of a very few people he likes. Listen carefully to what I say. You will undoubtedly try and ingratiate him by word and deed. That will get you nowhere. His unspoken response will be here is another little wimp trying to break into my family."

"I'm sorry but I don't understand what you are trying to tell me.

"What I am saying is that the only chance you have of winning his approval is for you to stand up to him at every occasion. Prove to him that you are as much a man as he is. This may not improve your chance of getting his approval. But the other way will definitely lead to his trying to destroy you."

At that very moment Valerie burst back into the room.

Anthony nodded at Mrs. Morrison, "Yes, I promise you I will beat Valerie each day so that she knows who the boss is."

"Mother, my friend is obviously covering what you really told him. Can you advise me of what really went on here?"

"Of course I will darling. He promised to return to our house as often as he can, so I can enjoy his company many more times."

"Obviously, Anthony, my mother is lying. Could you tell me the truth?"

"But there is nothing that I can tell you other than what you mother just spoke of."

Valerie simply nodded, knowing neither of those two would be honest with her.

But before Anthony left, Mrs. Morrison had advised him that their door was always open to him. In fact, she looked forward to more of his visits.

Upon hearing this news Mr. Morrison just nodded his head. Normally when his approval was not sought out before an action was taken, he would flare up into one of his famed fits but, surprisingly, not this time. He merely had Valerie arrange for a private meeting where he could meet and chat with this young suitor of his daughter.

Mr. Morrison was a powerful and monumentally successful man. His businesses and his family were the only things Mr. Morrison really cared about.

He had hoped for a boy as his first child but that was not to be. Valerie's birth had been a difficult one but, determined to have a male heir, Mrs. Morrison was soon pregnant again. The baby was still born and she nearly died in this birth-giving disaster. The doctors suggested they never try to conceive again.

The answer, for Mr. Morrison, was to lead a life that led to a long series of mistresses or pure prostitutes. He never again bedded his wife.

"Have him here two weeks from tonight. I'm sure all will go well with this young man you are so enthused about."

Valerie managed to get word to Anthony about the brief delay they must face. "But Father will be most pleased to meet with you."

Ecstasy gave way to increasing tension as the days flew by, and there was no response from Anthony.

At breakfast on the fifth day since Anthony had made an appearance at their home, her mother rushed hastily into the breakfast area while waving a piece of paper.

"What a lovely young man. He has just written me the sweetest note and asked me to pass it on to my husband and tell him how much he was looking forward to meeting him."

Finally the night of the meeting arrived. Everyone was extra special in their politeness to one another.

"That was a glorious meal my dear. Now may I drag this young man into my office, so that he and I can speak about what great men we are?"

All of them laughed as the two men disappeared into the extra large room Mr. Morrison called his office.

He first poured a scotch for himself and then offered one to Anthony who promptly turned it down.

The men took seats not two feet apart as Mr. Morrison next offered Anthony a cigar.

"No thank you, sir. I have just not learned how to handle a cigar as yet, maybe someday I will."

"Nicely spoken, my boy, I'll remember those words. Tell me something. Have you ever wondered how I managed to put together this massive company of ours?"

"I would be lying to you if I didn't tell you that I did do some research about it when I first met Valerie. And may I offer sincere congratulations to you on what you have achieved."

At this point Mr. Morrison changed his countenance as he leapt from his chair.

"Well, that is the first bright thing I have ever heard from you, and I'm glad you did so. I also did some research on a chap named Anthony Angus Donnell. But, despite my hiring an expensive group who specialize in that sort of work, they were not able to find anyone bearing that name."

He stubbed his cigar out in the tray on the table behind him and with a little more anger coming forth he said, "But they did find a scrubby youth from Cork who seemed to have a remarkably similar name. Do you happen to know that wastrel?"

Anthony instantly knew that their battles were about to accelerate.

"I know that name very well. It was mine for the first seventeen years of my life. I decided right then and there that I didn't want to have anything more to do with being Anthony Angus O'Donnell. And, by the way, he was far from a wastrel.

He was about to stop, but the glare from the obviously angry man facing him triggered the advice Mrs. Morrison had given him – 'Stand up to him, or you will immediately be the loser.'

"I do believe if you knew what it was like being an O'Donnell, you might understand him a bit better. Did they tell you that I swore that I would be as successful as any man could be? I assure you I will achieve that goal."

"As a matter of fact, the one positive thing they relayed to me was that you had given up being the typical drunken Roman Catholic who populates Ireland. They could not find anything else worthwhile about you."

"With all respect, I don't give a damn what their report said about me, and, more importantly, I couldn't care less about what you may think of me. The only thing you should be concerned with is, do I love your daughter? I believe I love her as much as she loves me, and, with or without your approval, she will become my wife."

"An answer I should have expected. I don't think of you. I only think of Valerie. She is our only child, and I adore her. There isn't anything I like about you. Now we will end this conversation. If she continues to like you, we will have further talks but, I suggest very strongly, that you do some very serious thinking about what you may be getting into."

"Yes, sir, and if I continue to like her, then we will have a rationale for our continuing this chat."

Without saying goodnight, Anthony turned and strode back to Valerie and Mrs. Morrison.

"I've had an interesting chat with your father. Valerie. If you want me to continue seeing you, you know how to reach me. Goodnight, Valerie, and also to you as well, Mrs. Morrison."

With that Anthony swept out of their home.

Chapter Thirty Six

The message from Valerie reached Anthony the very next day. Coincidently she asked that he be at their home in exactly two weeks, which was the evening of his college graduation.

The letter then dropped its formal tone and pleaded with Anthony to be there promptly at seven, as she was desperate to have a few words alone with him before her father appeared.

The evening arrived, and Anthony waited outside her door until his pocket watch advised him that it was seven o'clock. He then knocked on the door and, to his surprise, it was opened by Mr. Morrison.

"Good evening young man. Let us go directly to my office and then we can join the ladies afterward."

Again the offering of a scotch and a cigar, and again they were both turned down.

"Good. I like consistency."

Anthony had prepared for this meeting and wasn't the least bit nervous. If anything he was in a fighting mood and was prepared for whatever would come forth.

"Well, young man, as I am sure you understand, you have passed a very important test. My daughter does indeed like you enough that we are having this meeting.

Anthony did not respond but sat there with arms crossed waiting for what else awaited him.

Mr. Morrison took a good swig of his drink and a long puff on his cigar waiting for Anthony to speak, but nothing was offered.

"Do you not have anything to say?"

"No, sir. My appearance here tells it all. Obviously, I feel strongly enough about Valerie that I am here to hear what you have to say. When you have spoken, I am sure I will have a rejoinder."

There was no way he was going to start their relationship in a subservient position.

"All right then. I think it is important that you know I think you are an arrogant and rude young man. I don't believe you deserve the honor of her liking you. But that is her mistake. She seems to care quite a bit about you. So I am allowing you to continue seeing her."

"Thank you. I too want to continue seeing Valerie. As to your thoughts about me, I believe I told you them the last time we met. Valerie liking me is of great importance to me. You are wrong about me, but that is your option."

"Indeed it is, and it is going to take much effort on your part to change my opinion."

"If I find it is worth my while to do so, I will try, but every word you speak lessens the possibility of my doing so."

Anthony was pleased with how things were proceeding.

"I heartily suggest that you do not continue this arrogant stance. I am not one to have as an enemy."

"Sir, you leave me no room but to fight you. You have done nothing but demean me from our very first meeting, and you continue to do so tonight. If things go well with Valerie, I will marry her -- not you. So we will live on without any mutual respect."

Again, more swigs and further puffs and the cigar was stamped out. The whiskey was put down and the man sat facing Anthony.

"Indeed we shall. But let me tell you how we are to survive. First, if I allow that marriage to occur, you are to join my company as an apprentice. That I insist upon. Should you decline that offer, you will never marry my daughter."

Morrison then went on in great detail about how trying it would be for Anthony to survive that period. That he would advise everyone in his company about how Anthony got the job and that, without a doubt, they would all resent this interloper.

"As my words never surprise you, so do your words never bother me."

Morrison ignored Anthony and merely continued with a further explanation of what Anthony would enjoy once he joined the company.

"You won't have a friend you can relax with. Every word and action you undertake will be berated. And, most importantly, you would never rise up to any other position but that of a lackey. I do not treat adversaries kindly. And if you survive all of that there might be some small future for you with my company."

"Mr. Morrison, you do not have the slightest idea of how tough and smart I am. Not only will I survive anything you force upon me, but even you will one day realize what an asset I can be. Furthermore, I intend to eventually take over your company and make it into a far more successful company than you could possibly imagine."

The two men stared at one another. Obviously cut of the same cloth, both were extremely confident in their ability to triumph in any war and at ease with that fact. Peace would never reign between the two.

Chapter Thirty Seven

The following weeks proved particularly trying for Valerie. At first she and Anthony were permitted to meet but once a week. No matter what event they attended, or if they just stayed at home, her father saw to it that their only child was always accompanied by a chaperone.

After a month of seeing Anthony only fleetingly, she had enough of that inane ritual.

At a quiet family dinner she was beyond mad. Her father was boasting, as was his want, about another company they were about to gobble up. In the midst of his dull explanation of what he had done, she suddenly threw her soup spoon at her father.

Her father picked up the spoon and started waving it at Valerie when his wife shouted out, "Richard put down that damned spoon, and for once in your life listen to your child. I totally agree with everything she is going to say, and if she doesn't get her way, then both of us will be leaving you."

Morrison was beyond astounded at this outburst.

Valerie had leaped to her feet as she screamed out, "Oh what a great man you must be. The world is your oyster, but you don't credit your only child with the ability to do anything. Well, dear Father, that is over."

Her mother quietly beamed. That afternoon, in a private talk with her daughter, she told Valerie that she must fight her father's strictures now, or she would soon lose Anthony.

"How am I to discover what I want if, on the rare nights I can see a man I like, he and I are chaperoned to death and cannot even speak to one another? So I am going to contact Anthony and tell him I would like to see him as often as he can get here."

"Valerie, you just listen to…"

"No, for the first time in your life, I want you to listen to me. Do you think you can handle that?"

Her father continued glowering at her.

"Anthony and I have strong feelings for one another. We want to do things that we want to do, and we don't need anyone monitoring what we do. Our current meetings are created by you. If we continue this charade I will probably lose Anthony and you will most certainly lose your daughter."

His face was as red as can be, and the anger he was dealing with was choking him. Many moments passed before he slowly put down the spoon and quietly said, "Fine, we shall do anything that makes the two of you happy."

There was no happy reconciliation for anyone at the table. All knew that the warfare would continue.

Inwardly there wasn't a happier young woman in the world. Anthony was everything she had always prayed for. She finally met someone who was bright, who made her laugh and kept telling her how fortunate he was to have met a woman as beautiful and intelligent as she was. His words of praise made her stand taller and smile continually.

Anthony was beyond delighted when he got the message that he was more than welcome to Valerie's house at all times, and no chaperone would be part of their meetings. At first it was twice a week but each week the number increased to the point where each Saturday, if he wished, he could spend the night at their home.

An afternoon in the park always included a gentle kiss or two. Valerie delighted in same and longed for more but Anthony would not allow it.

One afternoon they were sitting in the large garden behind her house. Mrs. Morrison was going on about the varied flowers that surrounded them as she sat some ten feet away with her back turned to them.

Ultra quietly, Anthony slid close to Valerie and handed her a folded note. It wasn't until long after Anthony had left and she was preparing for bed that she read what he had written.

'I am going mad. I want so much to hold you, to kiss you and show you how much I love you. I can't continue in this manner. If you care for me as much as I care for you, let us ask your parents to allow us to marry.'

The next week Valerie told the man she loved that he was to meet with her father two days hence.

As both expected, it wasn't the pleasantest of meetings.

"Well you seemed to have won this first skirmish, and I wish you well. But, starting this Monday, you will appear at my office and begin your apprenticeship. Will you be there?"

"Thank you and, yes, sir, I am anxious to come to work for you."

"We shall see. If after your first month there you still desire that position, we will have a family meeting about the possibility of a marriage between you and my Valerie."

Two months later an announcement went out to the family and friends of Mr. and Mrs. Morrison inviting all to the marriage of their daughter, Valerie, and the honorable Anthony Angus Donnell.

Stephen Blake, Anthony's sister, Grace, and three friends from college were the only invitees representing the Donnell family.

Because he was so new on the job there was no time for a honeymoon.

That decree came down from his immediate boss, Mr. Peter Steele, who was the toughest, meanest man Anthony had ever met.

"Are you jesting? You don't know shite about what you are doing here. Maybe in a year from now you'll be given a week off."

A teary plea from Valerie to her father yielded a stern approval of the decree handed down by Steele.

"I'll tell Steele to allow him the Monday off after your wedding."

Valerie wanted Anthony to leave the company, but he would not do it.

"No, I don't quit battles. I win battles. Your father and I will be warring for a long time. This is going to be a long term affair, and I am going to enjoy everything they dare to throw at me."

The marriage was held on a Friday night. By Monday evening Anthony had taught her all that marriage could bring them. Valerie had proven that she was ready for anything Anthony came up with. There was a time when she just loved Anthony, but now she worshipped him for the wonderful new world he took her to.

Chapter Thirty Eight

Of course, the newlyweds lived at the Morrison mansion, but they managed to have the third floor overhauled to where it was their tiny but comfortable home.

Only rarely did they share meals with Valerie's parents. Learning to cook became a prime occupation for both of them. It was a chore they delighted in.

So yes, Anthony was happy at home, but the days at the office were pure hell. The first day he walked into the office, he had been introduced by Mr. Morrison with the following: "This is my son-in- law. He is joining the company. Give him something to do."

Mr. Morrison rarely uttered anything else to or about Anthony.

The consequence was that he was hardly ever addressed by even one man in the office. He was never given anything of worth to do. In essence he was treated as a brainless lackey. Result? A constant boredom that was slowly poisoning his mind.

Anthony managed to separate his near perfect life with Valerie from his bare existence with his father-in-law. That relationship was as it was promised to be. During each of his six-day work week, all went the way Morrison wanted it to be.

On the other hand, Sundays were a paradise gleefully shared with his wonderful wife.

Valerie lived a love-filled life that was marred by only one problem. Anthony was constantly barraging her with advice on the 'proper way' to do things. On her good days, she attributed it to his nervousness about being a married man. On her bad days, she wondered if he really did love her.

The fact of the matter was that he loved her far more than he believed he could love anyone.

What really caused these outbursts was his desperate need to prepare her for the days he would need her as he conquered the world.

Yes, she would bring in much money when that was needed. But more importantly, she must know that buttressing his every action was as vital as the money. They must be at all times as one.

More to the point, what they did always was to be his way.

Peter Steele and many of the others seemed to delight in giving Anthony as much hell as any man could handle. For Steele it all got down to one sentence, 'Beat the shite out of him.'

Anthony took every stupid order set down by Steele as if they were gospel, and not once would he complain.

On the contrary, he would take whatever chance he got to thank Steele for all the 'good' advice the man gave him.

He learned all he could about Steele including the fact that he had three small sons who he adored. Anthony often came in with a big bar of chocolate for the boys. It was not too long before this campaign began to work, as Steele was only vicious to Anthony when others were around.

"You know, he really isn't a bad kid. And I think he has a lot in the brains department, but every time I try to tell Mr. Morrison something nice about the kid, the boss tells me to keep the pressure on. It is driving me crazy."

The pattern of dealing with Anthony became the standard on how to handle 'The Kid.' Give the kid a break when Morrison was not in the office and treat him like a stupid peon when the boss was there. It wasn't a pleasant way to spend one's days.

Slowly the word was seeping out to all the staff that if Anthony was 'accidently' killed, the killer would receive a pay raise.

Some two years had gone by and Anthony had not moved an inch up the ladder. He was the perpetual apprentice, but he would not concede that he had lost the battle.

The boredom that assaulted him each day was a pain that hurt more than anything else. He found refuge in constantly repeating his unrelenting mantra, 'I'll kill the bastard before I give in to him.'

What above all irked Anthony was that he would come up with idea after idea on how to do something more efficiently or suggest how to co-op a rival company in their battle for a lush piece of business.

Each of these ideas was laughed off or just not considered. Yet, more often than not, his idea would be slightly altered and put into action. Of course, no credit came his way.

The tyrannical Mr. Morrison treated him, be it on or off the job, like an errand boy.

Morrison felt he had justification for his tyrannical attitude towards all people. Starting with nothing but a cunning mind he had built a business empire of formerly Irish-owned enterprises, and it had been a brutal job. They ranged from simple financial loans, to worthy individuals, to sophisticated banks and to several accounting and management companies.

Put together, they were a powerful economic entity. He had done it all and was damned proud of what he had accomplished.

What neither Morrison nor Anthony realized was that each of them followed the same ethos, 'Destroy or be destroyed.'

As the end of the second year approached, Anthony had hardly moved up the ladder more than an inch or two. Being in the man's presence was rapidly building into a cancer-like disease.

His yearning to kill the man grew with each day. The deliciousness of the thought grew stronger each passing moment. The planning for the event seemed to draw the event closer and closer to reality.

He began to think kindly of his own father whose only disease was stupidity and an addiction to liquor. Mr. Morrison, who hardly drank at all, was besotted with the assurance that he was God's gift to the world.

The only time Mr. Morrison behaved like a human being was on Sundays in church. The smile on his face lasted throughout the service, and when a thought came forth during the sermon that particularly appealed to him, he would even nod kindly to Anthony. It was his way of telling Anthony to 'Listen up, you little fool, you might learn something.'

And, as they left the church, all were accustomed to waiting patiently as Morrison glowed while he and the Vicar chatted away.

The imbalance between six days of horror and one day of pure delight was like having a knife plunged into one's heart and then having it extracted just before death finally came.

One weekday all changed. Steele came towards Anthony and tossed a letter on his tiny desk.

"This is a first. It's a letter addressed to you!"

The return address showed that the letter came from Father Michael McGuire. The address was that of a little church not far from Dublin in the tiny town of Enniskerry.

Chapter Thirty Nine

Anthony must have read the letter seven times before he decided what the words meant. At first he believed the words as they were presented.

"I am sorry, my friend, for acting so maliciously back at Trinity. Thoughts of those days have been plaguing me for some time now. I am sorry for being such an arrogant and demanding buffoon. I hope you accept my apology. Please forgive me."

The two-page letter carried on in this self humbling manner. Towards the end of page two, the words turned into what Mike was now doing and how much joy it had brought him.

The final paragraph went on about his not being able to get away from his duties at the church, but if Anthony could steal a few hours any late Saturday afternoon, Mike would like to make the apologies face to face.

At the seventh reading, it dawned on Anthony that it was an invitation he could not turn down. The letter was just Mike's way of saying that he missed Anthony and that he was a happy man who wanted to renew his friendship.

Yes, he would go to this never heard of town. He would tell Mike of the lovely home he and the beautiful Valerie shared. He would go on to fabricate the great advances he had already made in the business world, and, above all, how great it was never to worry about money.

That night he told Valerie of his dearest friend Mike who was a Priest in Enniskerry, a small seaport town north of Dublin.

The fiction began with his statement concerning the rationale for the trip. Apparently one of Mike's parishioners was getting too old to run his successful boat construction business. Mike, knowing of the big company Anthony was associated with, realized this might be an opportunity for doing a good deed for two people.

"I really don't think Mike has a clue about business, but he was a good friend in school, and I would like to oblige him with a visit. I'm sure your father would not be interested in it but, then again, who knows. It would only be one Saturday, but I am sure we can make a fun day out of the trip.

"But darling, how are we going to get there and back?"

"Well, I have a crazy idea. I know your father bought one of those things that seem to be replacing horses. I haven't seen one. In fact, I am not certain what they are called. Do you know what I mean?"

"Do I know? Whenever I see my father all he talks about is that noisy and smelly thing he just bought. He is such a snob about it. If he tells me one time more about the man he hired just to drive him here and there, I will shriek at him. He calls him his chauffeur, whatever that means. Enough about that silly thing, it does sound like a lovely little trip. When would we do this?"

The conversation was going exactly as Anthony had planned it.

"Enniskerry is fairly close to Dublin and I am certain, if you asked your father for the loan of that thing and its chauffeur, he wouldn't turn down our having some fun on the coast. I think the only time my friend would be able to see us would be this coming Saturday."

What Anthony did know was that Valerie's mother had been planning a large event for that Saturday. It was a huge flower show and, as she constantly declaimed, 'Everybody will be there and we will earn a huge amount of money for the charities we support.'

"Oh no, then we cannot possibly go. That's when Mother is having that wonderful flower show. Did you forget Mother going on and on about it"?

"Darn it. I did forget it."

"Darling, Mother will kill me if I don't attend her major effort of the year. Why don't you just go visit your friend, but come back early enough so that we can have dinner and a wonderful evening together."

Triumph as planned. Each little victory at home bolstered his ego. All of his despair and vain battling for recognition on the job was washed away. He would be free for at least one day. Happiness loomed ahead, and he could not wait to set Mike straight about how grand things were for him.

"I would love it, but I would definitely need the transportation your father can supply."

"Not to worry. I'll tell him you invited me to go with you on this visit with a friend who is presenting him with what might turn out to be a very profitable business acquisition."

She then darkened her voice, glowered at him and in almost perfect imitation of her father said "So he finally does something that may be good for the company. What's the matter with that?"

Anthony collapsed in laughter as she went on, in normal voice telling her father that she had to be with Mother for her big event so she had turned down Anthony's request that she accompany him. The one problem that remained is that he did not have the means to get there and back quickly enough to dine with her.

Her father would undoubtedly say something like, 'Nonsense, I'll have my chauffeur pick him up real early Saturday morning and have him back home no later than five o'clock.'

And all Anthony had plotted came through as planned. He still had the golden touch.

Chapter Forty

Early that Saturday morning Thomas, the chauffeur, arrived to pick up Anthony. He could not be more subservient, as he ushered Anthony into the back seat of this awesome vehicle and tried to cover him with an expensive looking velvet blanket.

Anthony would have nothing to do with that. He had other plans for Thomas. At last he had someone who could become his friend, his ally. He declined both the back seat and the blanket.

Instead he offered the man his hand and in the friendliest of terms said, "Hi there, my name is Anthony, and I would really prefer being up front with you, if you would allow me to do so."

It was a full two hour trip to Enniskerry. The first thing he asked Thomas was to explain everything about this thing they were in. Thomas quite proudly became the master of the moment as he held forth about his pride and joy.

"First off you could call this an automobile or a car, either word is good. You happen to be riding in the finest damned vehicle in the world. It is a Benz Patent-Motorwagen. It is the first car to be made available throughout the world and still is light years ahead of all the others."

"And what makes her move?"

Thomas explained about gasoline and how that propels the car.

"There isn't a better moving car on this earth. But if you are going on a long trip like this one you must carry ample gas to get you there and back. Right beneath the back seat I have enough gas to take us to each coast and back."

Thomas was very proud of driving the car and didn't miss any detail about the motor, the lights, even the leather seating. He could have gone on forever but Anthony diverted him by asking how he managed to get along with Mr. Morrison.

"You really want to know that?"

"Yes I do. I trust you, and you can trust me, so I can tell you that Morrison is the bane of my soul."

Though Thomas had only been with Mr. Morrison for a few weeks, he already loathed the way the man had treated him.

"Well, I do trust you and thank you for bringing that up. That bastard treats me like I was a piece of trash, while he is a God or something. I'm a peon who must do everything but kiss his royal arse. If it wasn't so hard to get a job, I would have left him right off."

"You think that is tough. What would you do if you worked right under him and had to suffer him every minute of every day? And he's my bloody father-in-law. How will I ever get away from him?"

Nothing could be more of a bonding than a healthy agreement on someone they both hated.

Anthony then steered their talk to football. Anthony, was a big rooter for Manchester, while Thomas was a strong ally of Peterborough United. A quick wager of one pound was made between the two on the next encounter of the two teams.

By the time their football discussion ended, Anthony had scored again. Thomas was a strong pal and therefore a strong access to just about everything his father-in-law said or did.

Anthony further endeared himself to Thomas when they arrived at the quite small Enniskerry Catholic Church.

"Look, Thomas, it is silly for you have to wait here while I meet with my friend. Why don't you wander into town or do whatever you care to do, and be back here in say three hours?"

Each parted from the other with a smile on his face. Anthony set for the coming session with Mike and Thomas looking forward to the chance of meeting up with a lovely lass or two.

In a roar, Thomas took off and everyone in the town and the church heard the god-awful roar. It wasn't often that the local folk had heard or seen such a contraption. Both children and the adults went wild and surrounded Thomas, their new hero.

Chapter Forty One

Only one face burst from the church. Of course, it was Father Michael McGuire.

"When I heard all the noise, I knew it had to be you making a grand entrance."

With that, the man of God threw his arms around Anthony. He apparently was as big and strong as ever as he squeezed his friend so tight that all the breath was pushed out of Anthony.

"Hey, hold off there. Are you trying to kill me?"

"No, you oaf. I am just so happy to see you that I lost control. Wow. Was that your car?"

Anthony dodged the question about the ownership but was happy to casually toss off that it was just one of many cars his company possessed.

"I must say, Father Michael, that I am a bit shocked that you are dressed so casually. Don't you have to be dressed a bit more fatherly?"

"No. this is Saturday morning when I don't meet with any of my parish, and the friends I might meet with all call me Michael."

"So noted, Michael."

Arm in arm, the two former adversaries walked into the small church. Anthony stopped and his jaw fell open.

Father Michael picked up on his expression "Rather plain for your tastes, Anthony?"

"Well, Michael, truthfully, I haven't been in many Catholic churches but this one is beyond plain....its barren."

"Yes, I suppose you can say that. But we have a way of making this little space just beautiful. Each Sunday we fill it with needy people. They bring with it enthusiasm for their church and all is beautiful. There is no passive worship here but whole hearted reaching out as we honor God."

With that he dipped his hand in a little bowl to his right and made the sign of the cross.

"We have everything here for our devotion. They may be smaller and less ornate than larger churches, but let me walk you through our church, and you will see that we have everything that a church needs."

He then pointed out the nearby Paschal Candle. To its right there was a little cabinet that held the sacred oil, the chrism that was used in every baptism.

"That door just behind the cabinet leads to a very small room in which a soul may celebrate the holy Sacrament of Reconciliation. But let me take you back to our nave. I am inspired every time I enter it."

To Anthony it was just a barren room with seating for about some eighty people or maybe one hundred. The seats were all heavy wooden benches which looked like they were most uncomfortable. Inwardly, he was laughing as he hoped all of the services were short so that as little pain as possible was transmitted from seat to buttocks.

But to Father Michael, Sundays revalidated his faith in what his church did in helping his congregation find the strength to smile about the difficult life each of them was living. This was worth any sacrifice he needed to take.

"My time here has proven to be remarkable for me, but I've just heard that I'll soon be moving to a bigger church in Dublin. I hope I receive the same spiritual uplift at that church as I do at this little sanctuary."

Anthony walked ahead and now stood close to the most sacred part of the church. He looked skeptically at the small altar which was slightly raised. On it were three small chairs, an equally small table, and on the back wall, a huge cross.

"I have learned more from this little church and the wonderful people who occupy it than from any book I have ever read. But let me take you to my office. I am certain you will be overwhelmed by its spaciousness"

And of course his office could not have been tinier. There was room for the smallest of desks and two equally small chairs.

"Anthony, I know you are suspect of why I asked you to come see me. But, please believe me that request comes with the best of intentions."

"Oh, I wondered for sure, but I was so curious to see you that I was glad for the invitation, and I am glad to be here."

Father Michael responded with a huge smile and the news that he had told his housekeeper to prepare some tea but was totally uncertain as to when it would arrive.

"So tell me about yourself. Yes, I heard you were married and that you joined the company that your father-in-law owns. Have you taken over control of the business as yet?"

Anthony was going to launch into a large tale of how well he was doing at the firm and how happy he was with his life. But sitting opposite this man with such a sincere smile and who would not brag about anything, he was dissuaded to say anything but the truth.

He needed to hear more from his friend before he could report on his far from perfect life.

"I would really first love to hear how Father Michael is doing. I promise I'll tell all when you're finished."

"Fine, but it will be a very short tale. I've been here almost three years, and it has been a massive revelation to me."

He then went into great detail that everything he always dreamed of doing had been fulfilled in his stay at the Church. It was difficult at first due to the congregation's love for Father Flanagan who had preceded him.

"He was a remarkable man. There was not a soul in this entire town that didn't love him and come to him for advice. I'm not talking about just the Catholics, but everyone here."

He then went on to say how frightened he was to follow that man. No one spared him added angst, as each reported on what a great man Father Flanagan was.

The man himself spent one month with Michael, and each day was a learning day about what he had to do.

This sacred man had advised him that the most important thing to do was to gain the confidence of every soul he met. To do so he must become the best listener he could be.

"He also strongly urged me to never lie to anyone. I still recall the exact words he used when telling me that. 'They'll know you are speaking the truth, and no matter how much the words may hurt them they will respect you for that.' I have lived by that advice."

Michael went on telling Anthony how difficult the first months were when he formally took over the church. At times, he did not believe he was making any progress but, bit by bit, the tide turned. He began to believe he was reaching them when, one by one, they began asking for his advice on non-religious matters.

"Of even greater importance is what they have taught me. Each of them is suffering mightily. They have never known any good times. They are the poorest of the poor, but they sustain themselves with the love of God. They rely on their God. They cling to him as the one hope they have. They have totally convinced me that God is essential to happiness. It has been a great lesson for me."

"Does that mean that you haven't always, as you say, totally believed in God?"

"Until now, it has always been a battle for me. But I know there is no doubt in their minds. They need God, and they have God. And that is good."

"And you personally, is there any room for God with you?"

"I wake up every day with a smile on my face and a song in my heart. So God must be lingering around me. My parishioners may not love me as yet, but I love each and every one of them. I am happy and fortunate in every part of my life. Can you see that?"

"Not only do I see that, I envy you every minute of your days here."

"Hearing you say that is what I confess is the real reason I asked you to come up here. Now, that's enough about me. It's time for your story."

"One more question, Michael. What about women?"

"Dear Anthony, as expected, it didn't take much time for you to get to that. I will answer it, but first tell me something. I am certain that you are in love with your wife. But do you cheat on her?"

Indignantly Anthony burst out with, "Of course not. She is my one and only love, and I know she worships me, and I more than adore her."

"I knew that would be your answer."

"Well, let me add to that. My wife could not be better. She is my one love. I do not need any other woman. Our life together is a total joy."

"Then please accept the fact that my only need for love is satisfied by this church and all of those who patronize it."

"So accepted!"

It was now time for Anthony to relate the sad tale of the one major flaw in his life.

"My father–in–law, on the other hand, is the most insufferable, demanding bastard I have ever met. At first I thought he was just miserable to me but that is not the case. He is miserable to everyone. The entire company is terrified of him but, strangely enough, I am not. I know I cannot stay there under him, but I'm at a loss about how to get away from him."

"Why don't you just leave?"

"Well, for one thing, my wife is either five months or six months pregnant."

"And of course you haven't saved any money to fall back on."

Anthony merely nodded.

They both looked despairingly at one another.

A timid knock on the door and then it opened on the oldest, sweetest face Anthony had ever seen.

"Ah, there you are. Miss Theresa your timing is impeccable. You are also, as usual, a wonder. And it looks like you have cooked up a batch of my favorite cookies. Bless you for honoring us so. And this is my dearest college friend, Mr. Anthony Donnell."

"Well hello Mr. Donnell. Don't believe I did something special. That man you are sitting next to insists that these cookies are always here in abundance. But, it is still a pleasure to meet you."

"And it is my pleasure to meet you, and I can see you are the cause for that ring growing across his stomach."

"Oh no. the poor man hardly eats at all. He is also so busy helping other people that he can't find the time to take care of himself. And now, if you don't mind, I'll be leaving you two old friends to yourselves."

With that, this wisp of a woman disappeared.

Chapter Forty Two

The two men happily dug into their cookies and tea. For sometime, not a word was passed between them. It was Anthony who finally broke the silence.

"Okay, you've avoided my last question long enough. So, is there a woman in your life?"

"You don't let up, do you?"

Michael took a long sip of the now cool tea and looking directly at Anthony, he made the sign of the cross then softly said, "That was for you to believe what I am about to say."

He moved his chair as close to Anthony as he could. Then he took his friends hands and in his voice even lower said, "I am going to tell you something no one else has heard, and I want you to swear that you will never repeat anything of it."

Anthony was all but hypnotized by Michael's action, but managed to get out a very weak, "Believe me, I will never utter a word of it."

"For the first six months of my stay I never had a thought about woman. But since then I must confess…. I have been in love with…. another long pause…. I have been in love with over… with…over fifty-three women."

Michael almost fell off his chair as he stared at Anthony's face, which was a mixture of awe, amazement, and then acknowledgement that he had been had.

Anthony slowly regained his composure. He kicked the chair from under Michael while shouting, "You fraud, you liar. How could you have done that to me?"

"Every word I said was true. I am in love with every woman in my church. Now none of our affairs have been consummated as yet, but I keep hoping within the next decade or two I will have at it with at least twenty- six of them."

This reply got Michael ten really hard punches and the promise that the assault was just beginning.

"Okay, okay, I lied. Yes, I love all of them just as much as I love their men and their children. But there is no attendant passion."

Finally the humor of it reached Anthony and he joined Michael on the floor with a dozen smashed cookies underneath each of them.

"Will you ever forgive me?"

"Not only won't I forgive you, I am going to take an advertisement in your local paper that tells all about you being a priest renowned for his ability to lie."

"Please, may I pay for the ad?"

"Of course you can."

Slowly they rose and dusted themselves off.

"Anthony, I may be an annoying oaf, as well as being the biggest liar in the Catholic Church, but may I offer you a serious thought? If I am at all remiss, just cut me off and that will be the last you'll hear of it."

"You always were much smarter than I, so get to it. You know me well enough not to have to give me license to cut you off. That is one of my favorite activities."

"Fair enough. Yes, I've told you how happy I am, but that is not the whole of the story. I remember what you once told me. You said that we were both very much alike. That we both wanted to be leaders. And, you added that we would do almost anything to attain that position. You were right."

Anthony was hooked. Was Michael saying that the nefarious acts he performed each day were also part of his own repertoire?

"Pardon the use of your title but, Father Michael, are you sure you want to keep telling me of your wayward ways?"

"No. I think I, in all honesty, have left those wayward ways back in my pre-priest days. What I would like to tell you about is what I have discovered. I know it gives me great hope, and I think it could apply to you as well.

It was as if they were back in Mike's room at school. Anthony then picked up the discussion as he went into a lengthy discussion of what he had first discovered in Trinity. The facts were that there was no doubt but that they were far smarter than any of their class-mates and the second being that they worked far harder than all the others.

"What I am saying is that we were only interested in getting things going in the best way, which, of course, was our way. Whenever we put our heads to a goal we wanted to achieve, there was no doubt that we would outwit our competitors."

"Yes, I would agree with you but that was in college where I think we were the only adults in that school."

"That may be true in your world, but I really believe that the same dullards are as plentiful here as they were in college."

Anthony thought of his job and the stupid men who were above him, and no matter what he thought or planned to do, he knew that all would come to naught because of Morrison's edict of never accepting a solitary thought he came forth with.

"That is easy for you to say in your current world, but it is not the entire story in the killer shark world where I abide."

"But, Anthony isn't the world changing right before our very eyes? Every day morality, or science, or basic thoughts about how one lives their life are subject to change. Why can't we change our world as well?"

"Because the idiots above us control everything with a tenacity that I can hardly believe."

"Yes, I can accept that. But must I just accept the fact that everything I practice today has been rigidly practiced for centuries? And even the minutest of changes are forbidden by our hierarchy. Why Anthony? Why?"

Anthony readily agreed and added that he was certain that all religions were stuck in the same malaise.

"And if that is right, do I have to accept that every word my church preaches is pure gospel? Or must I, in some way or other, try to implant some fresher thoughts to my congregation that might help make every day a little nicer for them?"

He allowed Anthony time to mull over that and then pounced again.

"Look at that thing you drove up in. Don't you think that everyone in town who was gawking at it would kill to get one themselves. Was the man who was driving it any different from those staring up at him? Was he an intellect or some super being?"

Thinking of how easily he had manipulated Thomas, the answer was simply, 'Far from it.'

"Well there we have the conundrum. All I'm trying to do is to put a little smile on our congregants' faces. I want to teach them how to think for themselves. Tell me, how are you and I going to make small but important changes in this place we live in?"

"Don't fool with me, Michael. You have obviously thought this all through, and you are ready to spring it on me. So, out with it."

Michael started pacing round and round through the tiny room. He was obviously anxious to get the words out correctly but equally nervous about how they would be received.

He started by telling of Father Flanagan who had spent over twenty-nine years at this one church and who was forever cautioning Michael about never straying from the basic preaching's of the church.

"He was in his late fifties and the nicest of men, but when he left, I am certain he had never strayed one iota in all his years here. As a result, there was a feeling of lethargy, or should I say boredom, evident in all our services.

In the rare conversations with other clergy, he found very few who were ready to talk about anything that smelled of a new thought. All of those further up the chain answered all his questions with, 'It is the word of the Lord, and it has never failed us.'"

"Okay. And you will be the young priest who dares to pose opposite thoughts to the current ones. So where does that leave you?"

"No. I am now going to be the most brilliant advocate of whatever they believe in. But, inch by inch, I am going to get people thinking new thoughts. It will rise from the people, not the pulpit. They will change all in the manner they desire it to go."

"Fat chance of their ever wanting to accept any change."

"Undoubtedly, they will need someone to quietly plant seeds in their minds. That is what I am learning how to do. Of course, when I have captured that technique I will start using it on other priests. And I will rise up in the ranks, and someday I will have the Pope's ear. That is my real mission in life."

"And just how are you going to achieve that?"

"The hierarchy loves priests whose parishes grow. I am going to grow this church exponentially. The news about the priest who is a great salesman will spread. That is all I will need to get their attention."

Anthony noted the glow in Michael's face.

"Go for it Michael. Winning or losing is not the issue. Taking the ride is what matters and I envy you that trip."

Chapter Forty Three

A short walk through the adjoining area ended with a quick view of the church's cemetery, which in turn revealed head stones dated over a hundred years ago.

Little conversation was exchanged. They were both a bit spent from Michael's talking and Anthony's attempt to decipher accurately what his friend was saying. His envy of Michael was more than apparent.

As they turned toward town, they could see a huge crowd near a beautiful and large lake that split the town in two. It did not take much time for them to perceive that at the center, standing atop his car, was Thomas, lecturing those around him.

The first words they heard was Thomas warning the crowd not to purchase anything other than this grand vehicle.

"It will be the most efficient car you can buy and worth every pence you've had to cough up to get it for your town."

"Come on, Michael, let us turn off that blowhard and have him take us on a triumphant tour of the town.

Michael and Anthony were promptly ushered into the back seat and away they went. Within minutes, they had circled the lake and passed just about every house and shop of this lovely little village.

Throughout the approximately fifteen minute trip people would pour out of the shops, or swing wide their front doors, or raise high the big windows each house had. Every soul viewing this parade shouted out a greeting to Father Michael. The words would vary from warnings for him to flee from this god-awful thing or 'Tis a wonder to see you up there, Father.'

When they returned to the crowd, Anthony told Thomas to take each of them for a short ride.

"My friend and I are going to have lunch. Give us about an hour, and I'll bring you something you can eat on the trip home."

There were no serious words exchanged during their luncheon. To Anthony, a question lingered with him, *Is he really as happy as he says he is?'*

Mike's thoughts stayed with 'If he is that unhappy how can he go on with his life?'

They both agreed that this little visit had been a delight and they must do it again as soon as feasible. And they both really meant those words.

Minutes after finishing their meals, Anthony and Thomas made their last triumphant tour around the lake and headed home.

Chapter Forty Four

Anthony spent the early moments of the trip home thinking of all that had transpired in the few hours with a man he had hated for a short period and now realized was really the only friend he had. He was more than envious of Michael's happiness.

Yes, Valerie was as fine a wife as could be found. She was not only deeply in love with him but she also was entirety compliant with everything he asked, or should one say, demanded of her.

Money was not a need -- if she needed to purchase anything that was slightly steep, she would tell her mother of that need. The message would reach her father and the need would find a place in their home within days.

Her father would use his generosity to berate a husband that could not answer all his wife's desires.

Her immediate reply would be, 'Well if he received a decent salary he would willingly do so.'

Those words would only heighten her father's ever growing apathy towards Anthony.

Today's little excursion allowed him the rare luxury of enjoying himself while alone for the first time in over two years. Yes, Valerie was a delight but this was just Anthony, by himself, satisfying his own needs. A smile graced his face as he rethought all that had happened that day.

The next day he and Valerie attended church services without her parents. Valerie particularly enjoyed Sundays with a quiet breakfast just for Anthony and herself. They would then attend church, followed by whatever struck their fancy as a fun thing to do that day and night.

But when her parents were home, which was most of the time, they had to spend every moment of the day with them. This gave Anthony seven days of torture for the week.

This Sunday the older twosome had gone off on a business trip.

Normally Anthony had to join Mr. Morrison on these trips where he served as a personal valet. They were the worst days of Anthony's life. But, wonder of wonders, his servitude was not required for this current trip.

Anthony, while attending a Sunday service, was normally adrift throughout the service, but today he kept staring at everything in the church.

Saint Patrick's Cathedral, oddly enough, had been the progenitor of Episcopalian thought in Ireland since the early Eleven Hundreds. Its current edifice had been built in the following century and it still stood out as a glorious tribute to the Church of Ireland.

The wealth of its congregation was apparent, as was the money they poured into its maintenance.

There were five priests hovering on the altar at one time or another, and, generally, Anthony was exhausted by all the standing and kneeling that went on throughout the service. It was another servitude he could do without.

But today was different. Possibly, it was yesterday's experience with Michael because today he even listened to the sermons. And as he listened, a tickle of an idea started percolating in his mind. The percolating grew into a potential thought and then expanded into a 'why not' phrase and from there into an 'I know I can do it' inner shout.

This was a resplendent happy event going on all about him. He let his eyes flow through the audience that sat bedazzled by the magic spewing forth from the altar.

At the end of the service, he asked Valerie to wait while he chatted to one or two of the lesser priests.

"Why would you want to do that?"

"As you can see, the Vicar is overwhelmed with folks trying to get his best wishes, so I can't get to him"

He spent a half hour going from one young minister to the other, and his brain started exploding with one maddening thought. He knew he must see Father Michael again and as soon as feasible.

Chapter Forty Five

That afternoon he asked Valerie how long her father would be gone on his next trip.

"Anthony, you have one fault. You never remember anything. Don't you remember my telling you that both Mother and Father would be leaving next week for their annual trip to America and will be gone for at least the next three weeks?"

Truth be told, she had never passed on that message to Anthony. She had pleaded with her Mother to take her and Anthony on the trip, but there was no way her mother would allow a newly pregnant woman to take such a trip.

She didn't want Anthony to know she had been denied this glorious trip, so she just never told him of it.

"Hallelujah. For the next three weeks we are going to have a wondrous time together."

The words were fine for Valerie, but for Anthony it meant that he would find Thomas, and the two would once again be going back to Enniskerry.

That Monday, he located Thomas, and that night he sat down and advised Valerie that the people at the office were sending him off on some stupid mission.

"I might be away two or three days. I asked them if I could take you along, but they did not know how many others would be in the car. I'll kiss the thought of you every night, and I hope you do the same for me."

Thomas and Anthony set off early the next morning and arrived at their destination shortly before ten A.M.

There was no one to greet them, so Anthony told Thomas to just wait for him as he hustled into the church. As he burst through the doors he saw a long line of about twelve women standing patiently outside of the confessional.

Talk about being in the wrong place at the wrong time.

He gently tapped the shoulder of the last woman in line and whispered. "Is it Father Michael in there?"

She glanced at Anthony in his fancy attire and stared him up and down before, in icy tones, said, "Well who else would you be expecting to be there? We've run out of good fairies."

"I wonder if you could get a message through to him for me."

"Young man, each of us wants to get a message through to him, so bide your time and you'll be talking to him just as soon as I have finished talking to him."

The day wasn't going well for Anthony, but he accepted his fate and did not say another word.

Exactly one and a half hours later, the woman emerged from the booth and Anthony took her place.

Michael barely looked at the person at the other side of the screen. "And, a blessed morning to you, my dear."

One of the first things Michael had altered was the traditional exchanges of prayers. He did conform to making of the holy cross. And that was it for the remainder of the formal greeting.

What he wanted most to do was to put the penitent at ease. It had not taken too long for those who met with him to grow accustomed to a more relaxed reception as they confessed their sins, be they imagined or otherwise.

Now his first words came following his glancing up to see who was in the booth with him. He then generally asked how their family was, or did their second child recover from the cough they were suffering with?

And so he looked up and said, "And how is ...WHAT THE HELL ARE YOU DOING HERE?"

"Obviously, I am here to take confession with you, but I would much rather do this outside the confines of this booth."

"How many people are behind you?"

"I think there are two or three."

"All right then. You go back to the kitchen next to my office. Ask Theresa to prepare some tea and biscuits for us, and I'll be there as soon as I can."

It took Michael some twenty minute before he came storming into the office.

"First of all you are not Catholic, so why do you come here for your confession? Secondly, knowing you as well as I do, there is little doubt in my mind that it would take many, many days to listen to you confess to all your sins. Now, what are you up to?"

"Because you know me better than anyone else, and you are the only one I can talk to. Please hear me out."

Michael nodded at Anthony, and extended a hand that gave permission for him to talk.

Anthony started with how much he had been affected by their prior meeting.

"I tell you there hasn't been a moment that I haven't repeated word for word everything you told me. And the word that most affected me was 'happiness.' Hell, I don't have the foggiest notion of what the word means."

It was not easy to continue.

"I have never...No, I mean why can't I just...Why.... Oh, shite."

"Relax, Anthony. Are you trying to tell me that you are unhappy?"

"I am so unhappy that I can't even think straight."

"Well I do believe you implied all of that last week. Why are we having this visit?"

"Because I am in dire need of help. I need your thoughts for me to unscramble this puzzle that is driving me crazy."

Anthony started talking and didn't stop for over ten minutes. It detailed yet again how loathsome his father-in-law was. That every day in the office sliced at what little ego he had left. Valerie was a dream, but he could not tell her how deeply he despised her father. It would hurt her too much, and he could not do that to her.

"There isn't one person in the world I can talk to, other than Thomas, and that is small comfort for me. This past Sunday, I really started going mad."

There was no follow up to this. Anthony just looked as forlorn as any human could be.

"Anthony, don't stop there. My friend, I did not rush through three confessions in order to hear empty statements from you."

Anthony turned a puzzled face towards his friend but still said nothing.

The staring continued between the two.

"Okay, I have many parish duties to attend to this morning. I will gladly continue this empty conversation with you at some future date."

Ignoring those words, Anthony started speaking. "I've got something important to tell you."

At first, his reply came forth very slowly but, having released those words, the tempo picked up.

"I believe I have the answer to my problem. Truth be spoken, I think you gave them to me. The problem was how I get away from that bastard who controls just about everything in my life, and do so with his good wishes."

He then went on to talk of how the only place the man is halfway civil is in his church. Anthony detailed the grandeur of Saint Patrick's Cathedral.

"They have five ministers, and I don't think a one of them has a brain worthy of any respect. And that is my idea. What do you think of it?"

"Pardon me. What do I think of what idea?"

"God, does being a priest mean you are also a dummy? I think I want to become an Episcopal minister. All I am asking is your thoughts on that matter. Am I crazy, or is there the semblance of an idea there?"

Michael looked more than startled. His friend as an Episcopal minister? How could this self serving, self centered egotist of such intellectual and devious prowess represent God? The mere combining of the words conniver and God shouted out *'No, No, No it could not be.'*

But that thought was immediately replaced by 'If anyone could pull it off, it would be Anthony.'

"Why can't you just quit your job and go back to running your Dublin pub? Or, if not that, I would think there is many a job you can get in similar firms to your current one."

"You are an ass. I'm sorry I came here for your advice. Valerie would divorce me, or her father would have me assassinated. I've got to leave with the blessings flowing from both of them."

"Yes, I guess you are right, But a minister? Do you really believe you can handle that job?"

"That's why I came here. What the hell do you think? Can I handle all the attendant bull-shite, without really going mad?"

"Anthony, you can handle anything you put your mind to, but the decision will depend on your total acceptance or denial of what will be required of you."

There followed at least an hour or more 'if I can, you should'… 'of course, but you are so self-minded that'… 'is Catholic theology so different from the Church of' … 'at least you can have a wife'… 'why the hell does a wife or no wife bring happiness'… 'as I said last week…'

Each of the two kept peppering their friend with a stream of questions and near answers until Mike said,

"Enough. Please, in plain English tell me why you would even think of taking such a step?"

"Because I know Valerie's bastard of a father would delight in having a prominent minister as his son-in-law. Therefore, I could obtain almost limitless funds for our church, and everyone in our ministry would be cackling with joy about that bright young man in Ireland who desires to be a man of our world."

"And then?"

"And then, I will become The Anthony Angus Donnell I have always wanted to be. I will be the best minister who ever pushed the tale of God. I will be the most favored minister in all the world and, just like you, I will rise in my church to the highest position I can attain and put my imprint on all the souls that I preach the gospel to."

"Let me ask you one more question. And please, be totally honest. I need that honest answer and, you even more so, need that honest answer. Do you believe in what your church preaches?"

It took Anthony quite some time before he could reply. The two of them stood face to face without a word being spoken,

Finally Anthony spoke.

"I knew I was right to come to you for help. Yes, you are right that is the key question that I must answer honestly. But there is not just one answer. There are two answers. What I preach to the people will be exactly the message that the church wants me to preach. I do believe in it, for them. Do I believe in any of that myself? Honestly? Not a chance. But I can use all my wiles to advance any cause. Now, do you honestly believe in every part of your theology?"

"At times I find it hard to, but yes, the bulk of the time I do believe in it."

"And our differences, do they exclude me from being a good minister?"

"No, Anthony. Go for it. I think you will be a wonderful minister."

Chapter Forty Six

Anthony had been spot on. He did get home early enough to take his bride to their favorite pub where the host, Steve Blake, at the insistence of Anthony, joined them for dinner.

"Valerie, Steve, you two are the people I love more than anything in this world. So I am going to reveal something that I pray you will both approve of. You must promise to tell me only what you really think. I beg you don't say a word just to please me."

At first, Valerie and Steve started to giggle at Anthony's serious expression, but then they realized that the expression, if anything, had hardened and his eyes seemed ready to shed a tear. Their giggles were stifled and, instead, fear gripped them both. They were now frightened silly by the intensity of his words.

They meekly nodded their heads, waiting for a message of unknown magnitude. They didn't have a clue about what he was about to tell them. Would it be some monstrous joke or a thought that carried with it dire consequences?

All conversation ceased when a wonderful shepherd's pie filled with lamb and potatoes and a delicious bottle of imported Gorbruck's red wine arrived at their table. Both had been previously ordered by Anthony.

"Well, I'll be damned. I don't care how much you want to say something brilliant, Anthony, but I'll not hear a word before I devour this food and empty this bottle."

"Agreed, Steve, let's eat, drink and relax before we get serious again."

The food and drink could not have been better and, in record time, the delicious meal disappeared. Their waiter was astonished on how quickly they called him and asked that the plates be removed and told him that he was not to bother them further.

Minor mutterings from all came forth about this perfect meal they had just consumed and the wine was beyond acclaim.

Silence became the dominant mode until Steve proclaimed that it was time to stop playing games.

"Out with it, Anthony, let us hear it all."

"I never thought it would be this difficult to just say one sentence. So, here it comes. Valerie, Steve, I want to... that is I want to... Oh, shite!"

And then a torrent of words spilled out so quickly that neither Valerie nor Steve felt they had correctly understood him.

Steve was the first to recover.

"Could you kindly repeat what I think you just said?"

This time, oh so slowly, Anthony said again, "Valerie, I want to leave your father's firm and uh, go to a religious school and become a minister."

Steve and Valerie looked at Anthony. The blank expression on their faces was identical. Each of their mouths were wide open and drooping. Not a sound came forth.

"Let me repeat what I said. I want to....."

"No, we heard you this time. Let us digest them."

Not a word came forth from Valerie.

"You want to become a Minister and I would like to become the Chairman of the Exchequer....What in the hell are you talking about. And you expect us to come up with a reply to those crazy words?"

Anthony took Valerie's hand with his right hand and Steve's with his left hand. He squeezed both quite tightly.

"Okay, I'll spell it all out to you, and when you begin to understand, just squeeze back, and I'll shut up."

He then went on by saying he would, without a doubt, commit suicide if he had to remain working for Valerie's father.

"At first, I went along feeling that, in time, all would change. But to my total frustration, it has only become worse. I am drowning in the constant belittlement pouring down on me day after day. It was as if I was taking a sip of arsenic that would eventually kill me. I am sorry, Valerie, but I cannot take it any longer."

"Don't say another word, darling. Just know that I am with you where or how you want me to be. I love you for what you have just said. And you will be wonderful in anything you do."

"I was praying to hear those words. Your father will, at first, think he has beaten me and try to force me back to his company but that is wrong. We will have our freedom, my Valerie, and a mission that will allow me to grow and do some good."

Steve jumped in with a bear hug for Anthony.

"You know I am with you in whatever you want to do, but please let me hear a bit more."

"For almost a year now, I have been at the point of not being able to take another minute of being treated like an utter idiot. Valerie, you are the only thing I have ever really loved. I don't want to lose you, and I believe I now have the way to keep what I love and, in the doing of that, also alter your father's feeling about me."

Valerie and Steve still could not fathom where this was going.

"Now bear with me. Steve, you know my friend Mike McGuire. Yes, Valerie, the chap I spent time with this morning. He is a Catholic Priest, but he is also a dear friend of mine. And, he is the happiest man I know. Without even knowing it, Mike inadvertently steered me to the path I want to take."

Steve jumped in with. "And he brought this crazy thought to you?"

At first he gave me grief about becoming a parson, but the more I talked of how I felt, the more he urged me on. He gave me the final push when he said I could become a good minister."

He squeezed Valerie's hand as he told her of sitting in church the past week and how everything seemed so calm for everyone there.

It seemed that happiness had enthralled all around him, and then he recalled that even Mr. Morrison seemed happy on Sunday mornings. And then it hit him.

"There I was sitting in church and slowly a thought came over me. If even your father can be pleasant in church, why can't I get him to become my biggest backer in this new adventure?"

"You are absolutely right, Anthony. When Father gets home, just tell him of how positive you feel about life when you are in church. Apologize to him for the many arrogant words you have expressed to him. And in your last words explain how much you envy those young ministers."

"You are so right. I'll also add something like 'I think I could be of some value to you in that position.' I am certain he would perk up his ears at that."

Valerie's head kept bobbing in approval. "You can't fail. Father will go for your idea in a big way and then brag to everyone that you have finally listened to him. He thinks God has always blessed his doings, and to have a personal representative presenting his message directly to God would be the grandest achievement he could have."

Steve, on the other hand, remained dour.

"Tell me something that will convince me that this is a new Anthony you are talking about. Or is it that callow youth I once knew? If the latter be the case, I pity any church that gets you for its minister. Those poor folk clinging to your preachings won't know what will hit them."

"I deserve that question, and I will answer it in the most honest way I can. I will use every tool I have to gain control of everyone I preach to and, probably more importantly, every one of my superiors. But it will not be just for my good, but for all of us to spiritually prosper.

One could hardly call it a lie, for Anthony knew he could make everyone feel uplifted and at times rapturous. Would he be using those emotions purely for his own benefit? Possibly.

But no one would know they had been used. All would be elevated in their belief that Anthony was leading them to a better relationship with their God, and life would be better and more forgiving thereafter. No one would even imagine that the more things bettered, its real beneficiary could be Anthony achieving a goal that he wanted.

His answers from Valerie and Steve were exactly what he expected. She grabbed him to her and, for the first time in her life, gave him a big kiss with all the world looking onto that display.

Steve topped her by shouting out as loud as he could, "Get us another bottle of Gorbruck's right now."

Chapter Forty Seven

"This is my first night back, and I have a ton of work to get on with. Anthony, I gather you have some sort of idea to propose to me, so let's get to whatever that is, and I'll quickly resolve the issue for you. And don't take forever in getting to the heart of the matter. Not that I can imagine you are capable of saying anything of worth."

"You may very well be right, sir. Let me start by saying that this idea of mine has led me to want to apologize to you for being the stupidest, most arrogant young man I could have been. I hope you accept that apology."

"Fine, fine, I accept your apology, but don't think that is going to change my opinion of you."

Valerie jumped up with fire in her eyes, but Anthony took hold of her and forced her to sit without saying a word.

Mrs. Morrison quietly entered the fray, despite knowing that it could stir the flames only higher.

"Anthony has voiced something that warrants nothing but further listening. Please, Anthony, tell us what you have in mind."

"Thank you, Mother, and I assure you, sir, it will not take long for me to say my piece. If you dislike what I have to say, I will follow your lead.

"You are damned right you will follow my lead!"

"Of course, sir, but do not take that as my not following up on my doing what I consider to be of value with my life. I have done much thinking and have come to the conclusion that I am not worthy of working for your company. I hope you agree with what I am about to propose, but whether you agree or not, I shall resign my position there and become a Minister in the Church of England."

Mrs. Morrison, Valerie and Anthony stood there awaiting the response from Mr. Morrison.

None was forthcoming. He just stood there staring at this youth in front of him.

"Let me further add that I could rise to a position of some economic value to your companies."

Anthony had purposely added the last words as a lure that he knew would excite Morrison.

Mr. Morrison was obviously taken aback by all Anthony had said. He spent an inordinate amount of time just looking at Anthony.

Mrs. Morrison rose and went to Anthony. She embraced him with a huge hug and then the words, "I am proud of what you want to do. I know you will become a minister that will make us all so proud."

Her husband hardly heard the words.

"Young man, for how long have you harbored those thoughts?"

"Sir, I must confess that I have always loved going to church but never felt I was enough of a religious person to become a minister. Meeting with my friend at his little church awakened such good feelings that I now know that I must devote myself to the ministry."

"What if I say I don't believe anything you said this evening?"

"I would be quite sorry that you felt that way. What is more important to me is my love for Valerie. What we do will be entirely her decision. We could stay here, or she and I could survive as, hopefully, a minister and his loving wife.

"Ladies, Anthony and I are going to take a short walk. I have things to ask of him and much to demand of him. I don't care to have either of you privy to where that conversation takes us. We will have made our decision on our return."

He didn't waste any further time but rose from his chair waved at Anthony to join him and left the room.

Chapter Forty Eight

The two walked the first three streets without exchanging a word. Mr. Morrison pondering on how to explicitly explain who he was and what he expected of Anthony.

On the other hand, Anthony knew that he had won this little skirmish. It had been difficult but Morrison was hooked, and, bit by bit, he would become Anthony's tool to be used over and over again.

Probably, for the first time in their relationship, the older man addressed his son-in-law in a generous tone.

"That was quite a little speech you just made. How much of it was blarney, and how much of it was true, or was it all just to satisfy my ears?"

"Everyone I have ever dealt with has credited me with being very bright. I think they are right. I could have presented you with all sorts of lies but it was obvious to me that there was no way I could and hope to delude you with it. Did I polish some of the words so that you would like them? Of course I did, but did I mean everything I said? All of what I have said comes from the bottom of my heart. However, let me repeat one thought I proposed earlier. Can you see how this little adventure can inure to the benefit of the Morrison companies?"

"Why should that thought change my opinion of you?"

"Because you are a smart man, and I am certain you can see the many ways I can become the biggest asset your company has ever had."

"Why do you think you can do that?"

"With your money and my conniving ways, do you not believe that my rise in the church will be mercurial? Do you then not see a hundred ways we would be able to increase your company's profits."

"A typical remark from the must presumptuous little bastard I have ever known."

"That is undoubtedly correct. But let's give it a little more thought. Churches throughout the world are constantly scrapping for more funds. The higher one goes in any church there is constant batting to bring more funds into its coffers. What could facilitate that more than urgings from a prelate to one company to send funds to another company and receive untold blessings from the church for doing so?"

The pace of the walk had been slow, but, with that remark, it seemed to settle down to a crawl.

Morrison was following Anthony's advice and envisioning how strong the church was. Yes, he thought, we are talking about millions of pounds and innumerable companies that could be bent by church pressure.

"If I were Roman Catholic, I would be aiming for the Papacy. As a member of the Church of England I will be aiming at the highest position possible. I like winning almost as much as you do. I also know I will need you in the forthcoming battles."

"Anthony, my biggest problem with you is that I do not trust you. Yes, I too can see great potential in your thought. So let me tell you the deal we are going to make."

He then grabbed Anthony's arm and swiftly spun him around and pinned him against a nearby tree. Though much the smaller man, the pain he was inflicting took all the fight out of Anthony

"You want my backing in this scheme. You have it. Money, of course is never a problem but always a tool. It will be available whenever needed, but the first time you opt to do something that, in the smallest of ways could harm me, I will have you killed."

Another fierce twist of Anthony's arm almost brought tears to his eyes.

"And, do know, that is no idle threat but something I have been forced to do to some louts here in Ireland who thought they could swindle me."

"I presume you accept that what is good for the gander also applies to the goose. So what you say rings fine for me."

A final twist of the arm and then Morrison released Anthony.

Breathlessly, Anthony turned to his father-in-law and, with a smile on his face, told him that their partnership was going to be very profitable for both.

Oddly enough, Morrison extended his hand, though a grimace graced his face. Anthony, with a smile, shook the extended hand.

A fearsome team had just been born.

211

Chapter Forty Nine

That very next week, Anthony retired from any other duty other than to find the proper college to prepare for his entrance into the ministry.

Anthony wanted a college that promised a look to the future in which to find its strength. It wasn't too long into this search that he found Ridley Hall College.

Nicholas Ridley had created quite a controversy within the Episcopal leadership. He had opened his school with the statement that he was looking for students who would be anxious to help establish the Center for Youth Ministry which would grow into a training school for Christian youth.

It was exactly what Anthony was looking for. This school had opened just fifteen years earlier in Cambridge, England. Though not a part of that distinguished University, it was none-the-less heavily backed by same. It quickly took the role of the leading advocate of the Evangelical Theory.

Its first president was, of course, Nicholas Ridley who was the leading light of this approach to religion. Though very much of the Anglican faith, its cry was to broaden the Church's span to welcome all sorts of different thinking and different types of worshippers. It was a rigid battle to open up the minds and hearts, first and foremost, of the youth of

England and was the leading proponent of youth ministry, in which it would groom a new brand of leaders.

Its emphasis on youth leadership quickly struck Anthony as the only school that could give him the opportunity for growth that he desired.

Within two weeks of discovering Ridley Hall, Anthony and Mr. Morrison scheduled a meeting with the leaders of the school. Shortly thereafter the coffers of the school were increased by a sizeable donation from Morrison Industries.

Coincidently, the remarkable grades Anthony had received in Cork and Trinity allowed for his early admittance to the school.

Attempts at keeping silent the news of the funding proved futile, and soon all of England's church leaders were in awe of the money and the brilliant student that came as a package to Ridley.

Leaving Ireland for the more affluent world of Cambridge, England, brought great happiness to Valerie and Anthony. For the first time in their lives, they were really on their own and could make their own decisions.

He and Valerie found a wonderful apartment, not too far from the school. It had a huge kitchen, an ample bedroom for them and a tiny adjoining room that would become the bedroom for their soon to be borne first child, Dora.

The apartment meant freedom for the young couple. Though Mr. Morrison had preferred that they take a large space that had additional rooms for him and his wife on their monthly visits. That was turned down by Anthony.

However, the rental on this lovely edifice was covered by the companies owned by Richard Vines Morrison.

On each visit, the first thing Morrison did after kissing his granddaughter was to slip a sizable amount of money to Valerie. The company books featured a monthly item which was used in the pursuit of new business.

Anthony approached his stay at Ridley with a zealotry he had never displayed before. He was a bit older than most there and soon was its leading scholar and, by far, its student leader. Each of the scholars and professors at the school took to Anthony as if they had discovered a rare mint.

Anthony's skill at divide and conquer found a unique home at Ridley as word of his skills were spread throughout the Evangelical movement.

Any potential student body rivals to Anthony soon found it best to leave the school. Others quickly recognized the strength Anthony displayed and became part of his ever growing team. In the years to come, this small group of men led to an ever growing Evangelical movement.

Normally, a student waits impatiently for his first assignment. This was not the way in Anthony's case. Amazingly, queries kept pouring in asking about where he would like to practice. Each letter came with what amounted to treatises discussing the value of each church.

However, he made no commitments at all.

To Valerie, he confided that he was flattered by all this attention but knew so little of what would be right for them that he could not choose one over the other.

That summer they visited many of the churches that had need of someone like Anthony.

On his sixth such church visit, he entered the city of Bath, England. Instantly he recalled Steve Blake and his words about Jane Eyre and Bath. An hour spent in its glorious Cathedral, and Anthony knew this would be his base forevermore.

His impatience with staying at Ridley Hall did not come close to his non-working ennui at Morrison's but he was so fierce in getting to his real career that he finished in two years, not the normal three all other students endured.

His short term at Ridley's was happily accepted when all were advised that though he no longer attended the school, the funding for Ridley would continue at its normal pace.

The officials at Bath Cathedral were delighted to invite Anthony Angus Donnell to their ministry. Yes, four ministers were more than enough for its needs but the addition of an extra pair of hands was not to be sneezed at, particularly when that one seemed to have access to considerable funds.

Being fifth man on the totem pole was totally distasteful for Anthony. Though he was certain that Bath was the ideal place for him, it wasn't easy being the lowest ranked of the ministers.

It was particularly galling because he, Anthony Angus Donnell, quickly learned that, save for Canon Rupert Keyes, those ranked above him were all a bunch of backside-kissing ignoramuses.

Keyes, on the other hand was one to be respected and discrete with. Though he did not get to spend much time with the good Canon, Anthony was ever on the alert when with him.

Canon Keyes was respected as a most brilliant leader of the Episcopal Church and renowned for his wit, his knowledge of the faith and a strength in his convictions. He was not one to be fooled with.

He dealt with Anthony in the same manner he handled each of the other ministers who worked with him. But, Keyes was careful in his relationship with Mr. Morrison. He really held the man in great disdain.

He had dealt with many of these lovers and supporters of the church, but he was ever distrustful of how far that relationship should go. Money should be welcomed, just so long as it never interfered with church policy.

Chapter Fifty

Anthony was the height of discretion in his first months at Bath. Everyone adored the hard working, ever available minister, who never turned down a task, no matter how menial it was.

It wasn't until the first Christmas services were just days away that a ruthless letter about Charles Humphries, one of the senior ministers of the church, was received in the office of Canon Rupert Keyes.

There was nothing in the letter that justified the claims stated, but the story it posed was so inflammatory that Keyes felt it best for all concerned to meet and discuss what their course of action should be.

As the six of them gathered in his office, he, without any preface, read the letter to them. He had first consulted privately with Humphries, and assured him of his disbelief of all in the letter.

"Now, I need your advice and guidance. How would each of you suggest I handle this situation? Let me first tell you that I have complete faith in Charles. This is a cruel and vicious letter. I do not believe a word of it, but I am uncertain as how I should handle it."

Three of the ministers were beyond furious at this ridiculous piece of fraudulent literature. Their consensus was to ignore it, and it would die of its own accord.

"Anthony, you have not spoken. What are your thoughts?"

"Please, let me first tell you that I totally agree with the others in their characterizing this letter as pure drivel, but I have been trying to formulate what is the best manner in which to handle it. I, too, would want to ignore it, but that would leave us with another problem. What if the real writers of this horrid letter let it get out to our parishioners? How do we handle that?"

Keyes jumped right in.

"Yes. We cannot be passive about this. We all know how strong a minister Charles is. We also know that many fine churches would love to have him as their leader. Charles, the best way out of this mess is to see that you go off to some other fine church. We will miss you but your record will remain untainted and your further advancement assured."

For the first time since the letter descended on them, Humphries smiled, and of course, Anthony was acclaimed.

The Canon opened the Christmas service sermon with a dire announcement.

"With much sadness, I must advise you that starting the first of next month we shall be losing the service of one of the finest ministers I have ever had the pleasure to work with.

It took much time for him to speak again.

"Pastor Charles Humphries is leaving us after working here for many years and having played a major role in making our church one of the best in this country. We do so because he has been offered a wonderful opportunity elsewhere."

He had to raise his hand to quiet the noise that rose throughout the Cathedral.

"My dearest friends, this is going to be the shortest service I have ever given. Please accept what I am about to say. Despite Charles' willingness to forego the offer and stay on, I have urged him to take this very important position. We will sorely miss Reverend Humphries. With his departure, we lose a wonderful part of our church,"

He then nodded to the back of the altar where Charles Humphreys was seated.

"Dear Charles, do know that everyone of good heart will forever miss you. I know that I will."

He then spent much time letting that message sink in.

"And, on another far less pleasant matter, a most spurious letter was recently received at the church office. It was one long and scandalous lie. I advise those who wrote same letter that I, and the Bath authorities, are pursuing those culprits. We shall find them and they shall receive the strongest penalties possible."

He then for many moments let his eyes roam through the crowds looking up at him. Everyone seated there could see the fury that was contorting Canon Keyes face.

He took what seemed to be an extra long period of time to take a sip of water and then to wipe his brow.

And, without a word about the holiday, he turned and started to walk off the podium. After taking but two steps he turned back hoping to bring a touch of levity into this dour moment. He spoke directly to his friend.

"Charles, I must confess I will most miss your uncanny ability to teach so many of our bell ringers how to really make those bells sing."

A smile at his friend, another at his parish members, and off he went.

Chapter Fifty One

It was almost immediately after the service that he asked Anthony to join him for but a few words.

"Well, how do you think it went out there?"

"Not too well, sir, but I don't know if that message could have ever gone well."

"Yes, I agree with you, but that is not why I asked that you join me. You have a good mind, and I wondered if you were bothered by anything in the letter other than its obvious lies?"

"I'm uncertain as to what you are referring to."

Keyes went on to say possibly Anthony had not read the letter as many times as he did.

"What eventually gripped me was that how badly it was written. For one, the obvious spelling errors, and then the total disregard for even the simplest of grammar. Do we have anyone in this church that is so grossly stupid?"

"I wouldn't have a clue about that.'

"I have thought about calling in Scotland Yard to help us determine the truth in this matter. How do you feel about that?"

"It could be wise, but I would recommend against it. All this fuss will die away as soon as Charles has left Bath. The sooner we get back to our normal path the sooner we will all be happy again."

"Anthony, you could very well be correct, but may I add another approach to that letter. Suppose that the man who actually wrote that letter is very educated, and all the errors were very purposely thrown in. I think that letter could well have been written by me or you."

Anthony paused before responding. The good Canon had taught him a very important lesson.

"Do not try to fake your way past a bright opponent. Get on his side immediately."

"I must say that is something I would never have thought of but you could be one hundred percent correct. That is a brilliant thought, sir."

Keyes profusely thanked Anthony for the compliment and then added, "Obviously, I believe I can be totally wrong there. Or is it that I am frightened it could be one of us who wrote that letter. You and I should keep alert that such a letter is never written again.

With a solid stare at Anthony the Canon turned his back to Anthony and exited.

Anthony knew he had just been dismissed with the slightest of reprimands lingering in those softly spoken words. He had been done a huge favor by Canon Keyes. Whether it was planned or forced into, because of a lack of proof, could not be ascertained.

Chapter Fifty Two

It was just after three years later that Anthony was again told to come to Canon Keyes office. It was a highly unusual and unexpected call.

Canon Keyes was a wise man who used his position to grow old and beloved. Throughout his career, he was a tough man to fight against but also a wonderful proponent of what he favored. He was astoundingly healthy for a man in his late sixties.

He was also a firm believer in the role of a Canon. "To my thinking, a Canon should be a firm leader of his cathedral and not just an honorary position for some old priest."

And he was just that, a tough old man who ruled over his cathedral with a strong hand.

"Well, my young friend, I am certain that you have formed many opinions in your brief stay here. You have made it clear to all of us that you are a rather ambitious soul. I like that in those who work with me."

It had taken him little time to recognize in Anthony Angus Donnell an eager and somewhat evil young devil. Oh yes, Donnell had the charisma to almost instantly charm all of the parishioners but had garnered less favor from his fellow ministers.

Constantly testing this young enigma, Keyes kept dumping much of the church's lesser chores onto this troubling but gifted young man.

Of course, he kept a close rein on Anthony. He was more than aware of Anthony's propensity to spending an inordinate amount of time talking to the leaders and families of the more prosperous families of his congregation.

"Anthony, I am going to confide with you on some happenings that will shape the course of our church for many years. How you handle that information will determine in my mind how you fare here."

"I will handle what you tell me only in the manner you wish me too."

"Good, I am glad to hear that. First, let me advise you that a significant change is about to happen at our church. In the next few months, each of the three ministers more senior than you, will be, one by one, transferred to other churches. Reverend Manley, of course, shall remain as our head minister. How do you feel about that?"

"I will miss those who are leaving. They have taught me much, but I am certain you have your reasons for doing so. I honor and have only the greatest respect for Reverend Manley. I will enjoy working with him."

"Ah yes, spoken very graciously. It was almost word for word what I thought you would say. What do you really think of them?"

Anthony knew that honesty now was the only way to go. "I don't think of them."

"Now there is the rare but honest Anthony. Well, let me join in that honesty mode. I did this mostly for them, but also to see how you can shine."

"I won't disappoint you."

"I am sure you won't. By the way all the pews in the church need replacement. Do you know of any ways of covering the cost for that?"

"I shall certainly see that my father-in-law gets that information."

"What a grand idea. I would never have thought of that."

"Thank you, sir."

The game between them continued.

"I am well aware of your frustration in being a lower cleric. I will be replacing those who are leaving, but I am uncertain at what level I should bring in the new ones. I am considering moving you up the ladder. But you are relatively new to the ministry business, and it might be wiser for me to bring you along a bit slower. What are your thoughts on the matter?"

"Whatever you decide on would be fine with me."

After a pronounced 'hrmph,' Canon Keyes abruptly changed the course of the conversation.

"You puzzle me, Anthony. Yes, you are bright, and, yes, I do believe you are good for our desire to make changes in the church. You have gone very far out of your way to become the friend to all our church members. I commend you for that."

"Thank you, sir. I appreciate those words."

"What puzzles me is how many of them have come to me with questions about how honest you are in that effort.

And for goodness sakes you have been transparent in your wooing of my favor. And I, my friend, like many of our congregation, have that feeling as well. Why is that?"

The reply was pure Anthony at his best.

"You and they are correct in their mistrust of me. That is because I am most anxious to be a strong force in our church. That has been a problem for me all my life. I push too hard and people misunderstand why I do. I apologize for that, and I promise I will do all you suggest to alter my ways."

Keyes stared long and hard at Anthony.

He pondered about the glibness of this reply. He took many minutes before he decided to proceed.

"I have told you the first of two things I am about to do. The second is of greater import. You are not to repeat any of what I say to anyone prior to my making the official announcement. Can you handle that?"

"Would I not be a fool if I countered with anything but, of course, I can and I will."

"Well said. I must also have your word that you will relax your constant warfare with the world. Not in words, but in deeds. You can be a good minister and a big success with my backing, or you can be nothing without it. I know a small church in Ireland that probably needs you more than we do. But, I am willing to gamble on you."

"You have made yourself perfectly clear. I like the way you tied the pews in the church to my future."

"Further proof of how bright you are."

Anthony did not reply.

"You have the opportunity to become our dear Reverend Manley's number one assistant. He is a kind man who will overlook all your faults, where I will not. Make one error and I will be shipping you off to a small church in Manchester. Once again I ask you if you understand me?"

A nod of the head was all that Keyes needed to continue

"Good. Then we have a deal. By the way, Manley strongly advised me to advance you up to be his number one man, and I will do so. Now let me add to what I have told you. Within the next few years, I shall resign my position here, and I will put forth his name as the one to succeed me as Canon of the Bath Cathedral."

"This doesn't come as a surprise to me. I have hoped you would make that decision."

"Manley has worked long and hard for me. He is nearing fifty and has spent over twenty five years giving his all for me and our church. So relax in your conniving. Manley will be the next Canon of the Bath Cathedral. After that I couldn't care who wears that crown."

"It will be difficult for anyone to succeed you, but I am certain Manley will do as well as any one could."

"Yes, I am sure you are. May I advise you to bide your time, and all should go well for you."

This was said with a most stern frown on Keyes face. Anthony read it for what it meant, 'accept what I say or you will soon be off to Manchester.'

Chapter Fifty Three

Keyes never varied his plans. Four years later Manley was given the valued position of Canon of the Bath Cathedral. Unfortunately, he was not of the stature of his predecessor. By title, he ran this magnificent church, but in fact, its real leader was Anthony Angus Donnell.

Some fifteen years later, on the second Sunday of February, Canon Manley mounted the altar to deliver that day's sermon. He hadn't done so in many years, leaving that task to his number one man, Anthony Donnell.

Raymond Vines Morrison and his wife rarely attended services in Bath but, with prompting from their daughter and son-in-law, he was quite stiffly seated in his usual aisle seat in the fourth row.

Obviously, the Donnell family was expecting something unusual to happen this day, for Nanny Morrison was holding tight to her youngest grandchild, Molly, who was contentedly sitting there quite happily sucking on her thumb. Dora, the oldest, was aglow with a beautiful new dress. Arthur and George had been warned by their father not to do anything but keep their mouths shut and to remain perfectly still throughout the service.

Morrison's aching back, that could hardly bend, did not suffer the pew seats kindly. If anything, his aging body had made him even meaner than in his early years. He sat there thinking that damned kid sure as hell turned down my idea to cushion the front seats just to harm me.

It took many moments before Canon Manley could do anything but stare at the large group in front of him. The words, when they finally came out, were uttered with joy despite the hint of a tear flowing down his cheek.

"I have been at Bath since my early twenties. Being here with you for so many years has been a delight for me and my family. Knowing all of you has been a blessing for us, and I am certain God motivated all of your actions. So, with my heart filled with thanks today I must...."

And there his voice stopped working as the tears took command of his face.

It took a good deal of nose blowing and wiping of his eyes and face before his mouth began to work again and out rushed the words, "At the end of this June, I shall be retiring from this God given gift of being the Canon of the Bath Cathedral."

A roar of 'No's' thundered out from those he faced. Though he waved to them to quiet down, the entire church rose as one, and increased the volume of 'No's'.

Mr. Morrison, on the other hand, thought *'Well it is about damned time we got rid of the old duffer. We've done well these years, but we could have done better without his meddling in some of our ventures. He damned well better give Anthony the job.'*

Though the tears kept drenching Manley's cheeks, he loved hearing the roars of denial spinning back at him from the podium. After what seemed like hours, the noise slowly subsided.

One very elderly woman who was seated close to the altar then pushed her way to the aisle and, waving her cane, shouted out in a creaky voice, "We love you. Don't leave us!"

"That is the nicest response I could have expected, and I am flattered by it. But, Mrs. Martin, I will never leave you. And let me proclaim to all that I have always loved you."

At this point Anthony rose from his seat in the rear of the altar and joined Manley. He took Manley's hand and raised it high above his head.

The two clerics hugged while the room kept exploding with 'No's' and then Anthony turned back to the rear of the altar.

"May I explain that very difficult decision I just announced. What our church needs now is a younger man more capable of achieving the goals of a modern church. Would that I were still in my fifties, but that is not the case. Fortunately, we have among us a man who is much younger and stronger than I am. He is also as driven a churchman as has ever existed. He is what we need at the helm of this near perfect church."

Those words brought forth a hush from those in the packed room.

"The man I speak of has many times over these years been tempted by exciting offers to leave Bath. In fact, he has recently received an offer to move to a large church in London. In that case, as with all the others, he has opted to stay with us."

The worshippers still were uncertain about where Manley was taking them.

"Fortunately for all of us, he has been loyal and consistent in his refusal to leave Bath. His love for you and Bath has succeeded in keeping him here."

Manley then turned back to Anthony and beckoned him forward.

"As I am certain you must have suspected by now, and for the few who haven't, do know that I am offering the name of Anthony Angus Donnell to all responsible for naming our next Canon."

A much tamer burst of applause echoed back at him.

"Consider how responsible he has been in spreading our gospel and his successful efforts in improving everything at our cathedral. When you do, I am certain you will join me in offering letter after letter spreading our message, so that when we next talk about our new Canon, it will be about Canon Anthony Donnell."

Still, little to none response came forth.

"Would everyone here kindly join me in an enormous cheer of thanks for this man who has given more, devoted more and made all our lives the better for his presence with us."

He then beckoned to Anthony who joined him at the altar.

"Please, I do not want any ovation for me. If things work out so that what our dear Father Manley proposes does happen, I will be beyond happy. If it doesn't, I will still be eternally grateful to spend the remainder of my life working with all of you fine people."

And the beautiful church burst into a strong, but not overwhelming shout of acclaim.

"But please join me once again in offering our thanks to the best man who has ever lead this magnificent church."

With that, just about everyone in this huge building, were on their feet clapping, screaming out their love for Reverend Manley.

Manley openly wept at this response and turning to Anthony hugged him and raised his hand. There was little doubt in the auditorium as to who would become their new Canon.

Tears began to dot Anthony's face but the slight smile he wore betrayed his true emotions. He was not yet forty-one and without a doubt one of the youngest to ever be named the Canon of a most important church.

It was not long thereafter that he was officially offered the title of Canon of the Bath Cathedral.

He joyfully accepted the title and duties passed on to him.

For the next twenty-five years every major issue facing the Church of England was first passed on to Canon Donnell. With his approval, the edict became church law. Without same, the church knew the edict was flawed.

The Church of England accepted the fact that if it were to succeed in its monetary needs, it had best agree with its holiest priest, Canon Anthony Angus Donnell.

Anthony's being the chief financial advisor of said church pleased Morrison no end. His relationship with his son-in-law had hardly changed, but, for the longest time, Anthony's ideas, no matter how self-oriented, were never dismissed. On the contrary, every thought offered was eagerly adopted.

And Anthony kept thinking, 'I was right as a kid when I set my credo. Yes, Canon Donnell. Nothing matters but success.'

Chapter Fifty Four

He really had to shake himself awake this time. It was not uncommon nowadays for him to fall into a deep sleep on these pleasant Saturday afternoons he so much enjoyed. The fact of the matter is that it was more like early evening when he awoke, rather than the normal late afternoon. What surprised him was that no one had tried to wake him.

Then again, it had been over three years since Valerie had died and certainly none of his servants would dare to wake him. None of his children still resided with him.

Oh well, wasn't napping one of the benefits of being over seventy years of age and still being as active as he was? It was his firm conviction that these, ever more frequent, naps were a great contributor to his health.

That afternoon he had spent much time rejoicing within himself about his years of being a strong, young fellow, and, in the very next breath, he was a father who could do nothing but bring harm down on his own children. He recoiled from what had probably been the worst day of his life.

It started innocently enough. The demanding father combating his four young and over active children who had embarked on some game that grew in intensity until their silliness escalated to where it became an annoying bore.

Their apparent distaste for their father and their adoration of their mother was a perpetual pain to him, but that did not stop him from rebuking each of them for their being aware only of themselves and not caring a whit about others.

He had been trying to un-puzzle a problem that had arisen at the church between his two youngest ministers. He was nearing a way to handle it all, when an absolute roar reached him and kept growing in intensity.

Of course, it was his four children playing some inane game in the far reaches of the garden. The laughter and the screams kept growing as, chasing one another, the noise grew to an intensity that did nothing but further annoy their father.

He roared out at them. "You get that horrific noise away from here and into the house this very moment."

The younger three did just that.

Dora looked him straight in the eye and sneered, "Oh, has our lord and master been bothered by his horrid children? I don't know how we can make amends for that dreadful sin."

Dora, the oldest and most favorite of the children he had sired, could be as tough and as full of fire as her father. Which was what he most loved about her.

Theirs was a difficult relationship. Like him, she was very attractive. Her mind was, if anything, brighter than his.

They differed in two ways. She was full of love for most things, be it the kittens she was always bringing home or for the adoration she gave to her mother and her three siblings. Sadly for him, it had been years since she shared any of that love with her father.

The far more serious difference was that since her earliest childhood, she also suffered with the dire disease, Asthma. Her first attack had occurred when she was six, and since then the severity of the disease had kept her physically weak.

The disease had a long and torrid reputation which some claimed started in Egypt around the year 450 AD. Early in the eighteen hundreds, English doctors found that the long held belief that it was a disease of the mind was fallacious and that it was a troublesome and often fatal disease of the lungs.

Most people laughed at those doctors' reports, but Dora prayed mightily that they were right. She knew that if it were physical, there would be a better chance of a cure being discovered

When she was well, she could stand up to anybody with her bright mind and fierce tongue. But, on her bad days, her bed was her only companion.

Of the other three, Arthur, his second child was the most serious one. George treated everything his father said as one big laugh be it serious or not. Finally Molly, the youngest, was always adrift in some dream world of her own.

In his mind, Molly was much like his sister, Grace. She was the only child that he worried about.

Arthur, George, and Molly took their father's constant preaching at them with what could be called ease. But with Dora, he never knew when she would fly right back at him.

That day he could not recall anything of particular horror they had done, but the severity of tone directed at the children was harsher than usual.

Before turning towards the door, Dora swept low to her father and said, "Dear God, please excuse us for daring to disturb his lordship."

"Just one bloody moment, young lady. Who do you think you are addressing in that tone?"

"I thought it was obvious. Are you deaf?"

She, rather than run from his fury, pushed right against him.

"Dear Father, let me tell you something I have wanted to say for the longest time. You never stop lording over all of us do you? Everyone else in this house cows before you. Even mother lets you verbally beat on her. Not a one of us is strong enough, bright enough or tough enough to ever please this master father of ours."

She looked at him with a sense of scorn that could not be mistaken.

"Well, I am sick and tired of you constantly telling us what to do, how to do it, and beating us down about everything we do that doesn't conform to your sense of what is right."

It took Anthony aback, and he could not find the words to answer her. All he could do was start to raise his hand.

"Ah, are you about to embark on your father's way of solving problems? I've heard so many times about your father beating up every one in your family. Well, I am also sick and tired of hearing how you got the worst of it, and how you hated him with a passion that was unreal."

She turned from him as if she was finished and then spun right back.

"Well you have never hit us, but your tongue has whipped us far worse than anything else you could have doled out. I don't hate you, yet, but you better change the way you speak to me, or you'll soon learn what real hatred is."

With that last outburst, and the comparison to his hatred for his father, the Reverend brought down the hand and smashed it across her face. It wasn't the hardest blow that had ever been struck, but the suddenness of it, and his obvious furious reaction at being equated to his father, was akin to lightning streaking through the room.

The tears gushed from her reddened face, but she did not cry out. Nor did she slump to the floor. Contrary to that she stood even taller and managed to whisper out "Thank you, Grandfather. It is good to see you."

She had hurt him far more than she expected. A look of disdain crossed his face. He stared down at her, straightened up and strode back to his seat in the garden.

That night, Dora had the worst asthma attack she had ever undergone.

Molly crawled into bed with Dora and kept rubbing an ointment onto her chest just as she had watched her mother do.

Even Arthur and George spent most of the evening trying to ease the pain Dora was suffering.

The fury that Dora had raised in her father never slackened. Not a thought grew in his head about how she was suffering. What reigned supreme was the hurt she had inflicted on him.

His Dora, his love, and the one child he really adored never tried to mend fences with him, and he never forgave her for the insult she had flung at him.

The berating of his children did lessen to a great degree but their relationship with him was replaced by total silence. Dora never spoke another word to her father.

Chapter Fifty Five

The greatest of all pains was visited upon the good man in the winter of Dora's seventeenth birthday.

The weather was absolutely abysmal. Torrential rains or huge snow falls, accompanied by near freezing temperatures, was visited upon all of England.

In early February, Dora got a mild cold. It gradually worsened and that brought on severe asthma bouts. Doctor after doctor was consulted, but the disease kept beating upon her. She grew weaker and weaker, and but days before her eighteenth birthday, she was too tired to fight any longer.

Early that afternoon, with her mother and three siblings at her side, Dora managed to open her eyes. She looked at each of her favorite people and smiled at them. It was a weak little smile but she even managed to add to it a little wink for each of them.

And then she added, "Tell Father I asked for him."

She closed her eyes, and within the hour, Dora was gone.

Arthur ran to the church to bring the sad news to the Reverend.

"Go home, Arthur. I'll be there very shortly."

As the boy left the room, the Reverend's normally erect back collapsed into itself. The excruciating pain brought aches to every part of his body.

What was normally a three minute walk, today took almost a half hour to achieve. He reached the front door and started to slowly gather himself together. He straightened his shoulders and stood as tall as he could.

Step by laborious step, he slowly mounted the stairs that led to Dora's room. Her door was wide open and he could see his family gathered around her bed. Quietly, he asked if he could spend some moments alone with Dora. Without so much as a glance at him, the children crept out. Valerie placed a gentle kiss on Dora's brow and then followed the children out.

He slowly closed the door and returned to Dora's side. He picked up her hand and tenderly kissed each of her fingers. He fell to his knees, and in, the quietest of tones, told Dora that she was the most precious thing in his life. He went into detail telling her of the intensity of his love for her.

"I loved you so much. You were the only person I really cared for and, fool that I was, I never could tell you how proud of you I was. Please, please forgive me."

For a full half hour he cried as he knelt next to her.

Without even knowing what he was doing, he kept squeezing her hands. As the flow of tears started subsiding, he wiped away the dampness that engulfed his face.

Ever so tenderly, he placed both her hands across her chest. He kissed her on both cheeks and managed to tell her again how much he adored her and how ashamed he was for being such a failure as a father.

He slowly rose and with great effort managed to straighten his body. For many minutes he just stood there looking down at her and then he turned and headed out of the room.

As he reached the door he stiffened his body yet again, opened the door and left the room.

To his family, and all the others in his life, his words of contrition seemed to focus on God and the mistakes God often made.

He hid his hurt behind words of God taking Dora to be closer to him.

Silly little Molly wrapped up the moment, when, with tears engulfing her, said "Well whenever I pray to God, I'm going to tell him I need her more than he does, and he should hurry up and give her back to me.

His parishioners, behind his back, were saying, 'Oh sure, he loves his God, and I guess that is good. But, couldn't he have found a little time to love his daughter as well?'

The entire family collapsed. Sweet little Molly hid in a closet and would not come out of it. The boys seemed absolutely dazed, Arthur filled with anger, and George, who loved to chat away and laugh at everything, could not speak a word for many weeks.

Valerie suffered the most. She aged instantly and never did recover the vim and energy that at one time was the symbol of what she was. Dora's death had put a crack in her heart that would never heal. The pain stayed within her, though she never spoke of how much she missed her Dora.

She applauded each of Anthony's continued successes while the hole in her heart would, within the following few years, lead to her early death.

Everyone stayed as far away from their father as possible. He knew that each of them blamed him, if not for her death, then certainly for filling her life with so much sorrow.

The pain that tormented him did not reform his attitude, nor bring him closer to the others in his family. He, who had fought and won all but a few very minor battles, had suffered a defeat that he would never fully recover from, but, to all, he remained as tough and demanding as ever.

He yearned to see Dora's beautiful face and hear her voice shouting out at him. Even his Saturdays which had always given him hours of joy were now filled with regrets and self scorn.

But through all of his personal hurt, he still found solace in philosophy of win every battle you enter into.

Internally, he suffered everyday of his life. True to his character, he sought solace in intensifying activities that brought added wealth to the family's companies and to the church.

Of course his father-in-law had long since passed away. Peter Steele replaced Mr. Morrison and Anthony's influence became even more pronounced. All who followed Steele maintained that relationship with Anthony.

For many years he was, de facto, the chief executive at the Church as well as the company.

Externally, he was still the rigid, demanding Canon of the Bath Cathedral.

Chapter Fifty Six

Somehow, each of the remaining children, in their own way, managed to learn how to live with their father and his intolerable ways.

Arthur's hatred for his father grew from the moment Dora died. Upon rising each morning and each night, before going to sleep, he swore that as soon as he could he would leave the home governed by that man.

He, of course, did not know that he was swearing with almost the very words that his father had uttered so many years ago.

'I will get away from him or I will kill him, but one thing is certain, he and I will soon part forever, and there is nothing he can do to prevent that from happening.'

It was not until his senior year at Cambridge that he found the way to achieve his pledge.

The guide to this was his very best friend and classmate, Trevor Harrison. Trevor had been born in Bombay, India, where his family still lived. He had been sent off to Cambridge to secure an education and to meet a proper breed of Englishmen.

Arthur and Trevor got on famously, because both of them were as bright as can be and both had devilish senses of humor.

Early one evening, he came rushing into Arthur's room while wildly waving a small book in his hand.

"Memsahib, memsahib, I have a wondrous tome for you to read. I think this is the perfect book for you, as it was written by a kid who was born in India. He is now in his early teens, which would make you almost his intellectual equivalent."

"How about I take that book from you and shove it up your you-know-what?"

"No, I was just playing with you. You absolutely must read this book. One of my uncles is the Headmaster at a tiny school called United Services College which teaches Indian students the blessing of being able to speak proper English. Supposedly, its students are as bright as can be, and, in particular, he raved about the writing ability of a young student named Rudyard Kipling."

"And what has that got to do with my reading a teenager's drivel?"

"My uncle insisted that I read this book. Quite frankly, I too had no such desire, but, being the good nephew, I did so. To my delight it turned out to be a real winner."

Soon thereafter, Arthur picked up the small book, and two hours later put it down. He was amazed at how good the book was.

Anxious to learn more about the author of 'Stalky and Company,' he probed reference work after reference work and was astounded at the information he found.

Yes, the author was born in Bombay who, when he was five, was shipped off to England for better schooling. He was desperately lonely but found happiness while putting pencil to paper and putting story after story together. Each and everything he wrote brought forth amazing acclaim for one so young.

His father had gotten a job at a publishing company and, as an off-shoot of his position there, managed to place his son, Rudyard, in a summer job at a small newspaper, 'The Civil and Military Gazette.'

The editor of the Gazette, at the insistence of Rudyard's father, had earlier read the first works of the lad and was singularly impressed with his writing gifts. He quickly hired the young boy. The readers of the Gazette never learned that the paper's newest writer was only a teenager.

The two college friends were in a heavy discussion about Kipling's newest work when a wild thought hit Arthur.

"You know this place called India has just given me a great idea. Any country that produces a Kipling and a Harrison must be special. The younger one is brilliant and the older one can barely speak the English tongue."

"So what is your incredible thought, Mr. Genius of all times?"

"Just stay with me. Is India as wild and mad a country as I think it is?"

"I don't know what you mean by wild but it has many cultures which are passionately followed. Many different languages are spoken. And all that diversity is ruled by us Englishmen, who are far from the nicest of folk. Someday soon, I envision a revolution of enormous proportions going on there."

There was no response from Arthur. The little thought that was bubbling within his brain and growing in dimension with each passing moment, preoccupied his every thought.

Finally he grabbed the smaller Trevor and lifted him high in the air.

"Now, I want you to listen to me and listen carefully. I have just come up with an amazingly great idea. Your words about India caused it to explode in my mind. It is most certainly going to change both our lives."

"Would you kindly fill out that sentence, you blithering idiot?"

"Oh yes, I am going to fill it out, and you are going to love every word that I pronounce. Please let that great mind of yours dwell on the following. By mid- June when school ends, we will be boarding a boat bound for India and by late August, we will be residents of Delhi, India."

The look on Trevor's face was a combination of pure terror and abject fear.

"I believe I heard what you just said, but could you kindly repeat those words?"

Very slowly, Arthur repeated the words he had just spoken and then added, "Yes, you can come back here, if you care to, but as for me, I am going to become a fine citizen of that world and never come back to England."

Trevor regained the power of speech and squashed Arthur's dream.

"Haven't you led me to believe that you are virtually penniless and that might possibly throw a wrench into your mad plan? Wait, I must be wrong. You must be independently wealthy. What a fool am I to worry about that silly thing called money?"

Arthur knew his friend was right. He didn't have a sou, other than the small allowance given to him each week by his father. Yes, it would be easy to save most of that. But at the end of the day that would be just a pittance.

Job…how does he get a job…? What can he offer that might bring in some serious money?

"Help me, Trevor. "How can I put together some funds that mean something in just about six months?"

Realizing that his friend was serious about that inane idea, Trevor tried to come forth with something worthwhile. It was after much correspondence with his people in Delhi that Trevor Harrison rose to the challenge.

Within a month of their 'go to Delhi' dream was proposed, Arthur was employed by one of Trevor's uncles who owned an accounting firm in Delhi. Yes, it was a rather low, almost errand-boy job, but it paid the rent.

Spending money came from Trevor's other uncle who owned the school for natives of India who wanted to improve their capabilities with the English language.

Thus Arthur would work both days and nights with much happiness as he fulfilled his promise to flee from the tyrant he called 'Father.'

Of occasion, some summers, he would return to England for a week or two.

George, learning of his brother's plans immediately started to think of his escape. But he, who had no desire for adventure, instead started planning his escape to the riches of America. By his late twenties he had met and married a young American girl, much his junior. He never returned to England.

Little Molly could not understand why her older brothers, whom she loved so desperately, had left her so alone.

She never forgave them for leaving her alone and loveless, and she never forgave them for deserting their father.

In her early teens she had discovered that she had an ear for the French language. With amazing diligence, and the help of a fellow student just one year older than herself, Maxine Chalmers, she had become capable of being a teacher of the French language.

Loving Maxine, and Maxine loving her, was a natural though dangerous result of their friendship.

She, who had faced troubles from almost everyone, knew that her father had no one left but her to give him the love he needed. Early in their relationship she decided to tell all to her father. In pure innocence she had invited Maxine to share a lunch with her father.

Each of the young women confessed to their so unusual relationship.

"Father I know you, like everyone else, does not understand what Maxine and I have found. If it bothers you, we shall part. But, do know I have always loved you, and I shall continue to do so, no matter what you decide."

The Reverend looked at his daughter, and a slow smile spread across his face.

"I don't recall my ever telling you about my sister Grace. I loved her very much. You are much like her, and I love you as much as I loved her. So, Molly, and you too, Maxine, if being together will bring you happiness and, as long as you include me in that happiness, I can only wish you a glorious life together. Let me suggest, however, that you move to an area where you are not known and therefore can lead any life you like."

Of course these words were self-serving, but they were, by far, the nicest gesture he had ever made in his entire life. The Reverend knew that he needed Molly and Maxine far more than they needed him.

God must have been listening in to their candid conversation for, shortly thereafter, a lower grade girls' school in the lovely northern community of Chipping Norton advertised their need for teachers of English and French. Molly and Maxine filled the need.

Chipping Norton to Bath or visa-versa became a much traveled path. He desperately clung ever closer to her for the remainder of his life.

Chapter Fifty Seven

This was probably the last Saturday afternoon he would spend in the garden. He had dressed well and had even draped a heavy red blanket over himself. Never-the-less, the cold seemed to tear through all of those safe guards.

The huge pot of tea helped somewhat, but he wondered why he foolishly preferred staying outside where shivers were shaking his thinning body every other minute.

Though he desperately tried to bring up pleasant thoughts, none would stay with him. His soliloquies often brought him great pleasures but, more and more, they filled him with self recrimination. When they did so, tears would become his ever constant companion.

His thoughts of his children brought him mixed emotions of joy and despair.

He wondered about Arthur, who only wrote him most infrequently. The boy had advanced in all his activities in India and seemed totally happy there, with not a thought of returning to England.

The letters from George were even rarer. Yes, he had invited his father to his wedding, but the trip to the United States seemed much too arduous to even think of embarking on.

He gathered from George's sparse letters that his marriage was a blessing, but finding a decent job was difficult.

George's one delight was that he had stumbled upon a unique Sunday position.

For some time, he had served as a lay reader at his local church. This entailed delivering a sermon when the minister could not do so.

All this changed for the better when a couple named Adams moved into an enormous estate not too distant from George's little home.

Not a soul in this little hamlet had as yet even seen the couple, but everyone was gossiping about who they were. The story most accepted was that they were multi-millionaires, and the husband was a descendent of Samuel Adams. Of course, none of this was ever verified.

George was awestruck one Sunday as, for the first time, he noticed the Adams take seats in the very first row of the church. The resultant sermon was by far the best he had ever given,

As George was greeting the parishioners outside the church, the Adams greeted him and commended George on his sermon.

He thanked them, and in turn, told them of his father, who was the reigning Canon of the Bath Cathedral, and had taught him all he knew.

"He must have told me dozens of times that no souls are saved after ten minutes, so each sermon I deliver never continues after that ten minute limitation.

They all laughed and then Mr. Adams asked if George and his wife could come by their home for a bit of lunch.

Every dream George had ever dreamed of was fulfilled when they told him how impressed they were with his sermon. They went on to explain that being deeply religious, they were going to transform a spare building they had on their property into a small church. Not wanting to have to adhere to diocesan rulings, they wanted George to deliver the weekly sermon and thus avoid any higher church meddling in their affairs.

George had jumped on the offer, not only for the few dollars it would add to his weekly coffers, but also for the prestige it brought him.

"Everything you taught me about being a minister has worked wonders for me and my employers. I thank you for what you gave me, and I apologize for not having told you this sooner."

Molly was still his constant love and her visits to him brought with it great joy. No, he did not make the trip to Chipping Norton any longer, but she would be knocking on his door at least once a month.

So, all was well with his children.

He refused to honor any thoughts about Dora. They brought with them too much pain.

Chapter Fifty Eight

Today he had given himself a strong dressing down.

"Stop thinking morbid thoughts. Remember the good times. That will bring warmth and happiness to you."

All sort of events swirled in his mind but then a wondrous memory jumped into his mind.

He saw Martin Flarity crouching before a very stern English captain. All the boys, including himself, were pointing at Martin as his pants kept getting wetter and wetter.

The memory of that trip shook the Reverend as he heartily joined those on the boat in laughter. What fun that day, some sixty odds years ago, had been.

Anthony Angus O' Donnell slowly rose and rapped his red blanket tightly around his body. It took a lot of time to get to the garden gate. An awkward power had risen within him, and forced him to rise and head for the gate.

He started walking towards some unknown destination. His steps were slow as can be, but his mind kept urging him on. It took an inordinate amount of time for the good man to reach the water front, but never once did he even think of turning back.

He smiled as he looked out at the sea. He had always loved the water and it was good to look out upon it once again.

On this late cold day there wasn't a person to be seen at the seashore. Anthony looked to the right and then to the left until he finally spotted some distance away the small boat he and his friends would use for today's journey,

He shouted to them, "Follow me. There's our trusty boat waiting for us."

He sensed his friends racing just behind him each vying to be the first one to the boat, but Anthony was the winner. He fell into his warship and grabbed the oars. Ever so slowly the boat caught the tide and turned seaward.

There was little need for rowing as the tide gathered strength the further out it got. On its own accord the boat took a course away from the shore. There was no need for rowing, but the good Reverend kept shouting to his companions to dig those oar blades deeper into the water.

"Don't be worried, Martin. We are going to be the most successful warriors to ever venture forth from Cork. What's ahead is going to be just grand."

He was increasingly being taken over by a tiring weariness that seemed to halt his every movement, and then a moment's clarity brought to mind his favorite liturgy. He must have used this liturgy hundreds of times at the many funerals he participated in.

'Oh yes,' he thought, 'those words were so strong, so meaningful.' Without a pause he started chanting those favored words as loudly as he could.

Whether we live or die, we are the Lord's.

Christ died and lived again, so that he might be Lord of both the dead and the living

We know that we are a building from God, a house not made with hands.

We are eternal in the…in the.., heavens.

Though his voice kept getting fainter and fainter he was comforted by the words familiarity.

We will be with our Lord forever. We....will be....we will see....

We will see God as he is....

To you, to you O Lord... I lift up my soul....The Lord is my light and my salvation...salvation...salvation.... whom then shall I fear

But, he continued to falter in both words and strength. His head tipped down and his hands loosened their grip on the oars. But he would not give in.

He pushed the oars deeper into the water, and though the words came out somewhat disconnected and much quieter he continued chanting the liturgy he so loved.

Whether we live or....or whether we live...or...die, we are the Lord's and.... and Christ died and died and died and lived and... and....

He managed to pick up his head once again and from his mouth came the tiniest of laughs and the words of the rough and tough Irish lad he always remained, 'What a bunch of shite that is.'

Another tiny laugh, and then the oars slipped totally out of his hands and into sea.

His head folded into his chest while his silent mouth opened wide.

The tides seemed to pick up strength and the little boat quickened its pace.

Had he been alert, he would have been delighted at once again fooling all in the world. Only he would know the truth and could answer the foolish question, 'Whatever happened to the Good Reverend?'

A word about our Author

Herman Edel has led a long and diverse life. As a music producer he opened offices in New York, Los Angeles and London, England, where he partnered with George Martin, the famed producer of the Beatles.

He was also the Mayor of Aspen, Colorado, in the '80s.

As a very young teenager, he saw his first Broadway show and was hooked for life. Since then, he has acted in and directed many comedies, musicals and serous dramas. All, far off Broadway.

For many years, he was host of a Broadway Musical show on public radio entitled, 'On With The Show.'

Not too long ago he fell in love with writing. It has brought him more joy than, as he says, 'A bum like me deserves.'

Irish Slang

'Acting the Maggot' – Messing around

'Bang On' –Correct or Accurately

'Bollocks' – Testicles

'Culchie' – A person from the countryside

'Da' – Father

'Eejit' – A complete fool

'Fella' – Guy

'Gorta Mor' – Irish Potato Famine

'Gurrier' – A hoodlum

'Holy Joe' – Self righteous person

'Houlihan' – Goon

'Made a bag of' – Ruined everything

'Molly' – Homosexual

'Wiss' – Homosexual

'Ya' – You